DECEPTIVE VOWS

REVISED EDITION

Gary G. Tavares

GARY G. TAVARES

DECEPTIVE VOWS REVISED EDITION

Printed By Kindle Direct Publishing (KDP)

Cover graphics by Richard Anthony Evans

Published by Tavares Entertainment, LLC.:

Gary G. Tavares

Tavares Entertainment, LLC.

3320 S. Cobb Dr. SE #21

Smyrna, GA 30080

678-437-4496

ISBN: 979-8-218-73011-6

ACKNOWLEDGEMENTS

I first would like to thank the Lord for blessing me with this talent. I also want to take this opportunity to thank everyone who supported and believed in me during this journey. There are too many people to list in this book. Instead, I'll just say, "You know who you are, and I know who you are."

DEDICATED TO:

This book is dedicated to ALL domestic violence victims and survivors, past and present. May you find the courage to move on and the strength to overcome the problems caused by the abuse. For those who are being abused presently, may this book give you the courage to seek and find help before it is too late.

INTRODUCTION

Deceptive Vows is a powerful, thought-provoking, and educational novel that explores domestic violence. It is based on the play written and directed by Gary Tavares titled "Until Death Do Us Part." The play was performed in Oakland, California, in 2000 and was brought back for an encore presentation in 2001. Gary Tavares also wrote the award-winning screenplay adaptation, titled Deceptive Vows, as well as the award-winning short film adaptation, also titled Deceptive Vows. Although this story is fictional, it feels very realistic and believable. Before writing the play version, Gary visited a domestic violence shelter in Concord, California, and interviewed several survivors. Gary also did some research on domestic violence. The novel aims to raise awareness about domestic violence and to help save lives.

CHAPTER ONE

****

Patricia Robinson lies in her prison bed, staring into space. She is a medium-sized Black woman in her late twenties. Her hair is shoulder-length and braided back. She wears blue prison-issue overalls, with her number stenciled on the front and "Hanford Woman's Correctional Facility" on the back. The cell is small, containing a bunk bed and a toilet. Patricia does not have a cellmate.

She has several pictures of her mother, father, friends, and her now two-year-old son, Marcus. A rather large Caucasian female guard runs a stick along the metal bars to get Patricia's attention. Patricia merely moaned as she lay there in a fetal position. The female guard opened Patricia's cell and stood there waiting for her. She said, "It is time for your group therapy session, young lady. The other inmates, as well as the doctor, are waiting for you." "I told you all I don't need any stupid therapy!" Patricia shouted. The guard looked at Patricia and said, "I will not put up with your mess under any circumstances. Now you know I am not the one!"

Patricia jumped up as if a fire alarm had gone off. She knew better than to test her luck with this particular guard. She was large and intimidating, known for her assertive nature. Patricia stormed out of her cell. The female guard caught up to Patricia and escorted her to the class. Ten women were seated at a group of tables that had been brought together. At the head of the table is a gentleman peering over his glasses. The gentleman's name is Dr. Morgan, who is highly trusted and respected by all the inmates.

He is a black man in his mid-to-late fifties. He has a thick goatee and wears fairly thick glasses. The women who have recently started serving their sentences are easily noticeable. Many of them have fresh cuts and bruises from abusive relationships. Counting Patricia, six black female inmates and five white female inmates are present. The room was painted an awful green color. The guard sat Patricia down and continued to stand over her. There are three other large female guards at the session. One is Caucasian and the other two are black. "Patricia, we are all glad you were able to make it," Dr. Morgan said with a somewhat sarcastic tone.

Patricia mumbled, "I can't stand this shit!" The large white guard said, "Behave, young lady, or I will lock your ass up in solitary confinement!" Dr. Morgan put his glasses on the table. He shook his head and wiped the sweat off his forehead with a handkerchief. He told the guards, "Everything is okay and the situation here is under control." After all, Dr. Morgan had an established image and reputation with these women, including a reputation for trust. The prison guard did back off, Patricia, but very slowly. Patricia did not seem to be threatened by the guard.

Patricia's mean cold stare down at the guard was quite intense. Surprisingly, Dr. Morgan said, "All the guards in here are free to leave." He did not want things to escalate. One of the black female guards said, "Dr. Morgan, we do not believe you are safe here with the inmates alone." Dr. Morgan felt safe because no inmate had ever physically attacked him in all his years in the system. The guards would always stand outside the door, watching the inmates through the glass pane in the door.

After the four guards left, Dr. Morgan flipped through his papers and said, "It looks like we are up to Carol Witherspoon. Remember, we are all like friends and family here. No matter what happens outside this room, we are family here. The one thing that connects all of you is your past and your experiences with domestic violence. Therefore, we are not here to judge one another. In a way, I guess you help each other by sharing your experiences."

Dr. Morgan took several boxes of tissues from his bag and passed them around the table. There was never a shortage of tissue boxes at these sessions. Dr. Morgan peered around the table and said, "Okay, we will start with Carol and work our way around the table." Carol was a relatively small black woman, in her early to mid-fifties. She had a notable scar on her face from past abuse. Carol pulled a box of tissues next to her. She was nearly in tears before she even began to tell her story. The other inmates just listened and stared at Carol. It was so quiet you could probably hear a pin drop. Carol was one of the more senior women in the group, so she received significantly more attention.

Carol finally choked forth the words and said, "I am here for killing my abusive husband, John. I met him about four years ago in San Francisco. We got married after dating for about three months. At first, he seemed to be the ideal partner for a woman. About a month into the marriage, he started physically and mentally abusing me. One night, he got home drunk and started beating me. I had a nine-year-old son named Kevin from a previous marriage. He came out to protect me, and John started beating him like a man.

I was used to the beatings, but I had never seen John hit Kevin before. I guess I became like a mother bear protecting her cub. I ran into Kevin's room and grabbed his Louisville Slugger baseball bat. I struck John until he was motionless. I thought I had knocked him out, but when the paramedics arrived, they started doing CPR on John. He later died at the hospital from massive blunt force trauma to the head and skull fractures." Several women in the session needed to pass the box of tissues around during this frightening story. Even the doctor seemed unsettled by what he was hearing. Dr. Morgan asked a somewhat critical question.

Dr. Morgan was known for asking tough questions during the sessions. He asked, "Why did you stay in the abusive relationship?" At first, Carol and the other women looked at the doctor as if he were crazy. However, Carol did answer the question by saying, "I stayed married to John for five hellish years because I thought John would change or that maybe I could change him. Another reason was that I was afraid. My family lived clear across the country on the East Coast, and I didn't have any friends. I also had a son to think about.

Carol continued, saying, "I kept wondering where we would go and how I would provide for Kevin and myself. I didn't have any skills, and I had never worked before. Moreover, my husband was the sole provider. So, I was afraid to step out on my own." Dr. Morgan looked around and asked, "How do we stop the cycle of violence? What are some of the things you believe would help?" That was a question he was sure to ask at each session. Sharon Walker, a rather petite black female in her thirties, looked around for a second. All eyes were on her because she was next.

Sharon said, "Okay, I guess I'm up now, so I will tell my story. In my case, my husband just refused to let me go. He just kept on stalking me." Sharon continued, saying, "I tried everything to escape him. I even moved countless times. No matter where I went, he would find me. A restraining order was not worth the ink and paper it was written on. By the time the police got there, he was always long gone, and there was no way to prove he harassed me." "I blame the judicial system for not doing enough," she continued.

Dr. Morgan scribbled some notes, pushed his glasses up on his face, and scratched his head. He cleared his throat and said, "So you believe the judicial system fails to do enough to stop this problem, right?" Sharon Walker shook her head yes and went on to say, "One time my husband punched me in the eye. I had a black eye, which was swollen almost shut. Sacramento's finest came and took my husband away for assault and battery. Believe it or not, he was back out in less than seventy-two hours. I got sick of the physical and verbal abuse and left him. However, he refused to let me live in peace. As I said, he always would find me eventually.

Sharon continued, saying, "I felt that the police were of little help to me in my situation. He should not have been able to continue to stalk me, harass me, and abuse me. I felt the only way to get peace was to take him out." Sharon wiped her tears and continued. "So that is what I did. I pretended to take him back. I even moved back in with him. I took his abuse because I had a plan. I planned to poison him to death. I started poisoning him, and he died about two or three days later." Sharon snatched up the box of tissues and wiped her tears.

Carol Witherspoon tried comforting her, saying, "It is okay, Sharon, you can do this. Let it go, girl, and you will feel much better." Sharon continued and said, "Since I went after him, it was called premeditated murder. The sad thing is, I do not regret killing him. I knew he would never stalk or abuse me again. I have done ten years now, and I still do not regret killing him. I just regret doing time for it." Sharon paused for a minute and said, "By the way, I didn't say my name. I am Sharon Walker."

Dr. Morgan shook his head again and then spoke. He said, "Thank you, Sharon and Carol, for sharing your stories. Your stories were remarkable and powerful. Okay, it looks like we have time for one more story. Patricia, we are up to you." Patricia just sat there looking around for a few seconds and said, "I pass!" Dr. Morgan said, "Patricia, are you sure you want to pass?" "Yes, Dr. Morgan, I am sure! I don't have anything to say!" Patricia said a little more loudly. Carol Witherspoon stood up and said, "Ladies, you are not going to help your situation by holding on to the pain you feel."

Patricia said, "Will you people just leave me alone? I said I don't want to do this. Why can't you fucking people understand that?" Sharon Walker attempted to add to Carol's comment and said, "Girl, you just need to…" Dr. Morgan cleared his throat, interrupted her, and said, "We can't force anyone here to talk." Sharon Walker just fanned Patricia off and said, "Fine, it is her life!" Patricia jumped across the table and grabbed Sharon by her throat. She choked Sharon and yelled, "You don't even know me bitch!" Suddenly, all four prison guards rushed into the room and separated Patricia and Sharon.

They placed restraints on Patricia and Sharon and escorted them both out of the room. One of the black Guards looked at Dr. Morgan and said, "So, Dr. Morgan, now you know why we prefer to stay here." Dr. Morgan sat there, puzzled for a second or two, and said, "I am sort of in shock myself because this is the first time this ever happened." The larger of the black guards said, "We intend to make sure it never happens again. Not on our watch! I do not care if you have to do the sessions in their cells. The session for today is now officially over, and the women need to move out. Let's go, ladies; stand up and move out!" Dr. Morgan stood up as the women were all being marched out of the room and said, "I hope we can continue the session tomorrow."

CHAPTER TWO

****

Later that night, Patricia tossed and turned in her bed. She was having a nightmare about her husband, Andre. Andre approached Patricia. He had a very mean expression. Patricia began to back up slowly but ended up in a corner. As her husband approached, she raised her arms to protect her face. It was not unusual for Patricia to have these recurring nightmares about her now deceased husband. Sometimes, like that night, she would wake up out of her sleep screaming or crying out loudly.

Patricia then woke up suddenly and shouted, "No, don't hurt me! I will do whatever you want!" An Inmate from one of the adjacent cells yelled back at Patricia. She was not too happy about having her sleep disturbed by Patricia's screams. She yelled out to Patricia, "Girl, what the hell is wrong with you? Are you crazy or something?" A guard's voice echoed through the prison as she said, "Cell block C, ladies need to hold down the noise!" The next morning, a large black female guard brought Patricia to Dr. Morgan's office.

This time, Patricia had the wrist and leg restraints in place. Dr. Morgan straightened up his desk and said, "Please take the restraints off her." The Guard looked at Dr. Morgan with disbelief and asked him, "Are you sure you want me to do this?" The incident with Patricia, which happened only twenty-four hours earlier, should have been fresh in his mind. Usually, Dr. Morgan leaned in favor of the inmates. He could identify with them to a certain degree and felt sympathetic towards them.

The guard unshackled Patricia but then put the restraints back on and said, "Doctor, I think I'd better leave them on. Trust me, you will be glad I did. I just don't trust this one." The Doctor did not believe Patricia would give him any more problems. He thought that if he could gain Patricia's trust, it would be easier to communicate with her. He wanted Patricia to drop her guard and open to him. He felt it would be a little more difficult for her to open and connect with him while she was tied up in restraints. The guard said, "I am sorry, Dr. Morgan, but it's for your safety. I'll be right outside in case you have any problems with her."

The guard turned to Patricia and gave her a mean look and said, "As for you, young lady, don't you dare start any shit in here!" The guard turned to walk outside. Patricia sucked her teeth and flipped off the guard once the guard turned her back. Patricia could not stand the guards, and it seemed like they did not mind putting her in her place. Patricia did not feel she belonged there, which led to a lot of anger. Dr. Morgan said, "Hello, Patricia." Patricia did not respond, but she did look around the room.

She refused to give him eye contact because she knew how he could almost mesmerize you with his looks. Patricia was one of the only inmates Dr. Morgan had not cracked. He felt it would just be a matter of time. Patricia looked down at a picture that was sitting on Dr. Morgan's desk. The picture was of Dr. Morgan, his wife, his daughter, and his son. She stared at it for a while. All Patricia wanted was to meet "Mister Right," start a family, and live happily ever after. Her marriage was in no way the fairy tale she had hoped for. After all, she never got to see herself, her husband Andre, and their child in a photo together.

Dr. Morgan started the conversation off by saying, "Patricia, nobody is going to force you to talk about your story. If you prefer not to discuss what happened to you, that is fine. Telling your story could be beneficial to you." Patricia examined the picture for a few more seconds. She then asked, "Is this your family?" Dr. Morgan said, "It is my wife Julie, my son Jerry, and my daughter Cheryl. Why are you asking about my family?" He felt somewhat threatened, and he thought she was being a bit intrusive. "I don't know, I guess I am curious," Patricia said as tears started to appear in her eyes. It made her see what could have been her own family.

Dr. Morgan removed the picture from the top of his desk and put it inside one of the desk drawers. He did not want anything to distract or upset Patricia. He needed her to be focused on the session, and he wanted her full attention. He tried to get to the point right away. "I brought you here to tell you that I may have to release you from the sessions. I simply cannot let one person destroy this program. There has been too much success in other facilities with the program," he said as he peered over his glasses.

Patricia got angry and said, "I will be stuck in this hellhole for a longer time if you release me from the damn program!" "I don't have anything to do with that," said Dr. Morgan as he shrugged his shoulders and leaned back in his seat. "Dr. Morgan, what do you want from me?" She did not want to tell her story. Unfortunately, that was not what the state wanted. The state believed there had to be some sort of rehabilitation and intervention for any woman who had gone through what these women went through. They mandated the program, and frankly, Dr. Morgan agreed with them.

Although the program was relatively new, it was already showing positive results in other facilities. Some inmates who completed the course performed significantly better upon release. Some were able to be released earlier after completing the therapy program. "Okay fine! I will go through the session, but I do not want to do it with the other inmates yet," Patricia said with an attitude. Dr. Morgan was surprised at such a simple request. He did not care how or where Patricia told her story. Perhaps this was the break he was looking for. He knew that if he agreed, he could get her to tell her story.

Dr. Morgan scribbled down some more notes and then said, "So, basically, you would like to have private sessions, right?" Patricia nodded yes, as Dr. Morgan paused to think. He looked up at the ceiling, twirled his goatee with his fingertips, and said, "I can't make any guarantees, but I promise to see what I can do. Now, in exchange, I need you to promise me that there will be no more outbursts or violent behavior. I also want you to promise to share your story with the group. I am scheduling a time for you to return next Friday to share your story.

Dr. Morgan continued, saying, "This is our final attempt to assist you in completing the state-mandated program. There will be a heavy guard presence around you and the sessions, due to your unruly behavior. So, do you have any questions, young lady?" Patricia had one more question for Dr. Morgan. With his family's picture still fresh on her mind, she asked, "How old is your little boy?" Once again, he seemed reluctant and hesitant to discuss his family with the inmate. However, he did say, "My baby boy is eighteen months old. Now I am reminding you once more of our Friday appointment.

Dr. Morgan continued, saying, "And please try to stay out of trouble for heaven's sake." He signaled to the guards who were observing Patricia through the glass pane in the door. They came in and escorted Patricia out. Later that day, Patricia was in the cafeteria eating at a table all alone. Carol Witherspoon approached her with a tray of food and asked, "Do you mind if I sit here with you?" Patricia replied, "I don't give a shit where you sit!" Carol looked at Patricia with animosity. Carol had always been respectful to her. Patricia usually had a table to herself during meals.

The other inmates generally chose to give her some space because they felt threatened by her. However, Carol thought she could get through Patricia's thick skin. Her mindset was like Dr. Morgan's. So, Carol did sit down at the table with a bit of reluctance. She had a bone to pick with Patricia and wanted to cut to the chase. She said, "Patricia, what the hell is your problem? You keep running around here like that, and you are going to get beaten down or taken out. These women are not going to keep taking your shit." Patricia looked at Carol and rolled her eyes.

Surely, she was not directly challenging or threatening Patricia, but that is how Patricia perceived it. Patricia looked at Carol as if she did not know what she was talking about. Patricia talked even with her mouth full of food and said, "Look, I just do not believe that they can help me. Shit, do you think anyone here gives a damn about what happened to us? They don't care! You see, we are forgotten just like everyone else in this dump."

Carol paused a few seconds, pushed her tray of food aside, and looked right at Patricia. Carol was starting to wonder if she could even get to Patricia, but she was certainly not giving up. Patricia just shrugged her shoulders and said, "To tell the truth, I just want to forget about it. It hurts so badly, and I do not want to keep re-living it repeatedly." Carol said, "Like I said in the session, holding the pain in and just hoping it goes away will only be detrimental to you." Patricia finally broke down and said, "I am just confused and scared." It was almost as if Patricia was looking for someone she could confide in and tell her story to.

Hearing Carol's story earlier had a profound effect on Patricia. "Do you think you are the only woman who has gone through this shit? Every woman in the program has a story to tell. Some of their stories differ, while others sound remarkably similar, but they all have terrifying tales to tell. I am sure your story is just as terrifying as the rest of the women from the sessions, but it needs to be told," Carol reminded Patricia. Patricia looked doubtful and said with an unbelieving expression, "I don't know, I guess so."

Carol said, "You do not have to feel ashamed of what you did. I am sure it came down to you protecting yourself, and killing your husband was most likely self-defense." Patricia bent her head down as tears formed in her eyes. Carol knew that at this point, she was breaking through Patricia's thick skin. Carol handed Patricia her napkin so she could wipe her eyes. "I once tried to bottle up the rage inside of me. It tore me apart from the inside out, and I even thought about ending it all. I did not get any relief until I told my story in a group setting," Carol said as she started to get emotional. Carol had told her story many times at the sessions.

Carol had already completed the state-mandated program but chose to stay in it so she could motivate and change the lives of other victims. Patricia paused for a second to wipe her eyes. She shook her head and tried to hold back her tears. This was not the tough image that everyone in the prison came to know. Patricia turned her head away from Carol. She simply could not let Carol see the tears streaming down her face. Patricia said, "You don't understand. It does not make me feel any better to talk about what happened. It makes me feel worse."

Patricia tried going to one of those programs when her husband started beating her. Some of the women in that program were beaten half to death and had notable bruises, cuts, and scars. Just seeing them caused her to have terrible nightmares for weeks. After that, she never wanted to go into any domestic violence program. One of the Caucasian guards approached the table and stood there, watching Patricia and Carol with a mean look for a minute. "You two Princesses need to hurry up so the next group can come in and eat!" The guard yelled.

Carol picked up her tray and went to empty it. Patricia followed her to empty her tray. Carol patted Patricia on her back and said, "Girl, you just need to stay strong. Just remember that all those women in the program are not only victims. They are also like your family."

CHAPTER THREE

****

Patricia was escorted into Dr. Morgan's office by two huge black female Guards. They placed her in the seat rather harshly as she gave them a mean look. One of the Guards points at Patricia and shakes her finger to give Patricia a warning to behave. The two guards left, but their presence remains, as they peer through the door. "Those two big bitches don't scare me! If they took these damn restraints off, I would beat the shit out of them," Patricia said.

Dr. Morgan turned on his radio and tuned it to a soft jazz station. He turned the volume down slightly so he could communicate with Patricia, but he sort of acted like he was waiting for her to settle down and tell her story. He did not want to put too much pressure on her. "So, Patricia, are you ready to do this?" Dr. Morgan asked. She gave Dr. Morgan one of the meanest looks. She did not like the doctor's tone. She thought there was no way this man could be getting on her case, too.

Patricia did hear a little about him before he came to the facility, but it was all good. "Look, Dr. Morgan, I changed my mind about that," Patricia said. Dr. Morgan paused and looked at Patricia. He started tapping on the desk with his pen. He was agitated. "What do you mean you changed your mind? I had to pull a lot of strings to arrange these sessions for you. I don't have time for games. So, what is it going to be, Patricia? Do you want to do this or not?" Dr. Morgan said.

Patricia said, "I meant I am ready to tell my story. That was what I changed my mind about. Just hearing the other women tell their powerful stories of abuse convinced me to tell my story. I want to be able to change the lives of other battered women. I mean, I know it's the right thing to do." "Patricia, did you know that the Hanford Women's Prison would be at the forefront of domestic violence rehabilitation? We are only the fifth prison in the whole country to receive a program that rehabilitates domestic violence victims on this level. You and the other women are part of something special. So, do you want to tell your story to me now or at the group session later?" Patricia looked up at the ceiling as if the answer was there.

Patricia looked at Dr. Morgan for several seconds and then said, "I will tell you first. I think it will help me prepare to share it with the group. I guess you can call this a practice session." "I think that would be a good idea. Would you mind if I tape the session?" She was somewhat reluctant at first because she did not understand why a tape was needed for the session. She started rocking back and forth because she was nervous. Dr. Morgan said, "The tape is for my reference and informational purposes. Now, are you comfortable? I need you to relax and be comfortable." "I am fine, Dr. Morgan."

She said she was fine, but Patricia still looked rather uncomfortable, and Dr. Morgan needed her to relax. "I will be okay. I guess I just want to get this over with," Patricia explained to Dr. Morgan. Dr. Morgan pushed the record button on the tape recorder, spoke into the microphone, and said, "I am Dr. Morgan from Hanford Women's Correctional Facility. It is the sixteenth day of November, two thousand and two. The time is eleven hundred hours. I am interviewing Patricia Robinson, a victim of domestic violence, who is doing time here for killing her abusive husband."

Dr. Morgan gave Patricia the thumbs-up sign to signify the start of the session. She snatched up a few tissues to prepare herself for an emotional session. She paused briefly as she tried not to cry. She cleared her throat and said, "Well, my name is Patricia Robinson, and I am serving time here for killing my abusive husband, like Dr. Morgan said. I decided to tell my story in hopes it will start the healing process, and I figure it might help other domestic violence victims." Patricia wanted to take the Doctor back to the beginning, where it all started.

She closed her eyes and went back about two years earlier. She flashed back to that summer and the events leading to that fatal confrontation with her husband. Patricia had two best friends. Yvette and Vanessa were both African American women in their twenties. Both were very attractive. Vanessa was light-skinned with beautiful hazel eyes. She attracted plenty of brothers, but she ran them away with her mouth and attitude. Yvette had light brown skin and a short, Halle Berry hairstyle. They were pretty much like sisters, having grown up together. Yvette was the more mature one of the trio. She was happily married with a family.

Vanessa was somewhat wild. She was good to hang with because you always knew she had your back. If you were friends with her and someone messed with you, they would have hell to pay. She was not only the fighter of the group, but she would not mind cussing you out, beating you down, or even cutting you. The girls always tried to get together for lunch. They were sitting at a restaurant table outside, eating lunch and talking. The weather was quite lovely, as it usually is at that time of year.

A small flock of pigeons landed near their table in hopes of getting a meal. Patricia asked, "How is your husband, Yvette?" Patricia loved talking to Yvette about her marriage because it seemed like a big fairy tale. Yvette always seemed so happy, and her relationship seemed perfect. Yvette said, "You know, girl, everything is wonderful. We are doing fine, and the kids are doing fine too." Vanessa asked, "Yvette, can you hang out with us today?" "I need to get permission from my husband," Yvette replied. Vanessa and Patricia did not like it when Yvette's husband stood between them, having fun.

It would not happen all the time, but it did happen on occasion. Patricia said, "Are you serious? You have to get permission from your man?" Yvette said, "You two are not married, so you don't know that there are rules for being married, especially if you want it to work." "Well, I am single and ready to mingle," yelled Patricia with her hands raised above her head. Yvette said, "Patricia, while we are talking about my man, I should ask you, how come you don't have a man?"

"I am okay with being single. I am just waiting for a good, strong man," Patricia said as she took a sip of lemonade. "There are plenty of strong men here," Vanessa said as she chased the pigeons away. Patricia disagreed with Vanessa. She always had trouble finding good men and keeping them. "I guess she needs another thug in her life. That is her idea of a strong man," Yvette said with a smile on her face. "Patricia, I think you are looking in all the wrong places. You will continue to attract the thugs if you do not change your dating habits," Vanessa said. Vanessa looked at her watch and said, "We have about two hours before the new Tyler 'P' movie. You are going, Yvette, right?"

Yvette pulled out her cell phone, dialed her husband, and said, "Honey, I am with the girls, and we wanted to go to the movies…Okay, I will be home as soon as the movie is over. It starts at two and ends at three-thirty… Okay, baby, I love you, too." Vanessa and Patricia just looked at each other and shook their heads in unison. Just as Yvette said, they had no clue about marriage because neither of them had ever been married. "He said he did not have anything planned, so we can hang out today," Yvette said as she put her phone away with a big smile.

Meanwhile, Andre Robinson, a tall black man, 32, was tossing and turning in his bed. His bedroom was huge with large paintings on the wall. The room was painted all blue. He had a king-sized bed with satin sheets and pillowcases. He was having a recurring nightmare about his abusive father. The dream was from when he was about twelve years old. He was under the kitchen table, crying and trembling as he watched his father beat his mother. He darted from under the table, grabbed his father by the leg, and tried to bring him down. His father flung him off his leg. Andre stood up and charged him again, and his father knocked him down.

Andre's father stood over him, waiting for him to get back up. "You no good little bastard!" yelled his father as he reached down to grab Andre. Andre woke up and snapped up like the dead rising. He was breathing hard and was soaked with sweat. His alarm clock was ringing loudly. He took his pillow and threw it at the clock, knocking it over. He got up and started throwing things and tearing things apart in a fit of rage. He had rages and fits quite often. Generally, he had them after the nightmares, which were usually about two or three times a week.

Sometimes he would lie in bed for quite a while before getting up. Andre got up, reached into the nightstand, and pulled out a revolver. He put one bullet in the chamber and spun the cylinder. He then put the gun to his temple and pulled the trigger. Fortunately, it was not his day to go, and the gun only clicked as the cylinder turned. "Shit, shit, shit!" Andre yelled out as he began to cry like a baby. His pain from his past abuse was deep within him. There were many days, just like this one, when Andre wanted to end it all. He tossed the gun back in the nightstand, got up, and started getting ready for work.

Andre lived in a big house all by himself. He had been married before, but he was now a single man. Andre was in the computer technology field. He knew almost everything about computers, including how to repair them. He was brilliant and earned a good living. He had a lot going for him, yet at this point, he was once again single. He had two pictures of females on his bedroom door. They were headshots of his two ex-wives. Both photos had large red 'X' marks through them. They also both had darts sticking in them as if they had been playing a game of darts with their headshots.

Andre grew up watching his father beat his mother, and he was also a victim of his father's physical and mental abuse. The past abuse seemed to be taking a toll on Andre's relationships. He never sought help for his problems and chose to deal with them on his own. As he got ready for work, he routinely would have long one-on-one talks with himself. He even often answered himself. Alcohol was what he used to cope with his problems, and he would drink heavily at times. He could even be considered a functioning alcoholic. Andre believed that the alcohol helped him control the beast inside him.

If nothing else, it helped him deal with, or at least temporarily forget about, his past. It was as if he had a split personality. At work, he consistently performed all his tasks on time and was even named Employee of the Year last year. Women seemed to be very much attracted to Andre because he was tall and handsome. However, he was somewhat selective. He sought women he could completely control, and he had no problem finding them. He had been single for quite a while now, and he was ready to start another relationship. He did not like the single life because his loneliness only exacerbated his problems.

Patricia was staying with her parents for a while. The economy was in a poor state, and she was laid off for quite some time. She had just recently received the call to return to work, but she had already lost her home to foreclosure. Her stepfather, Charles, was a hardworking and strict man. He was a tall, dark-skinned man in his fifties. He looked young for his age, but his appearance was not in the best shape. He had short hair and a thin mustache. Patricia was like the daughter he never had.

Charles practically raised her from the age of six or seven. He was very protective of her, even now that she was grown. Growing up, Patricia would not dare bring a boy to the house. She was still reluctant to let her male friends meet her stepfather. Patricia seldom heard her mother and Charles argue. Charles pretty much was the king of the castle, and what he said usually went. She did remember her real father, Derrick, from her childhood. She used to watch Derrick physically and mentally abuse her mother for years. She tried not to dwell on it too much because it gave her nightmares.

Patricia's mother was single for a while after she left Derrick. After she left Derrick, she fell in love with a guy named Richard. Richard molested Patricia from the time he moved into the house. That turned out to be several years. The bastard even took her virginity. Donna did get engaged to Richard. Fortunately, Donna decided not to marry him. He started becoming a lot like Derrick, and Donna did not want to continue raising Patricia in that environment. Patricia never told her mother about the molestation. Her mother, Donna, was very easygoing and laid-back.

Donna was sort of old-fashioned. Donna was a short, light-skinned Black woman. She had shoulder-length, jet black hair. That was probably from the American Indian side of her. She was in her fifties, but still attractive. She grew up on a farm in the Midwest, spending a significant portion of her life there. Charles and Donna had been married for over twenty years, and he had moved her and Patricia from the country away from her family for a while. Now they were back near the city.

Their home was small with a fireplace in the living room. The smell of Donna's home cooking was in the air. They were all eating breakfast together as usual. Donna could throw down in the kitchen. Charles always praised her cooking, going back for seconds and sometimes thirds. "Damn, this is good, baby," Charles said while stuffing his mouth, licking his fingers, and reading the newspaper at the same time. "Well, don't get any on the walls or the ceiling, honey," Donna joked. Charles was always running behind in the morning, and Patricia was his timekeeper. He had to be at work by ten. "Daddy, you are going to be late again," Patricia said while pointing to the clock.

"By the way, I will be home late tonight because I need to catch up on some things at work," Charles said. Donna said, "I will have your food in the refrigerator waiting for you just like always." There were many times when Donna climbed into bed by herself when Charles had to work late. It wasn't too bad lately, thanks to Patricia staying there. "I am going over to Vanessa's house right after work, so I may not be here later either," Patricia said while loading another portion on her plate. "Well, I guess I will be here by myself. Looks like it will be a Blockbuster and popcorn night," Donna said sadly.

Charles said, "Patricia, make sure you call the house, Donna's cell, or my cell if you have any problems." They all had cell phones, and they had each other on speed dial. He often worried about Patricia when she stayed out late. In his mind, she was still his baby girl, and his job was still to protect her. Donna did not have a problem with Patricia staying out late. Donna thought Patricia was still a virgin and would stay that way until she got married. For some reason, Patricia was okay with her mother believing that. Patricia and Donna were close. Donna believed Patricia was still a virgin based on one of their woman-to-woman talks.

Charles was stretching and yawning as if it were the end of the day. He had a full belly now and was ready to go to sleep. "Honey, I will make your coffee strong and put it in your thermos so you can take it with you," Donna said. Donna's coffee was so strong you could almost stand a spoon up in it. It was pure rocket fuel, and it could wake the dead. She always made sure Charles took some with him to work. After all, she wanted to ensure he made it through the day since he was the breadwinner. Charles gathered his things so he could leave. He kissed Donna, then Patricia, and then headed out the door.

Patricia needed to leave soon, but she always made the time to help her mother clean up. She felt the least she could do was to lend a hand. She was pretty much living there rent-free. She offered to pay the rent, but her father would not agree to it. He told Patricia that she was his daughter and that he would not accept any money from her. She still managed to slide some money to Donna now and then. Donna was extremely frugal and could hold money like a pit bull. That benefited all of them because Patricia and Charles struggled with saving money.

Patricia gathered her things and prepared to leave for work. Donna stood between Patricia and the front door. She did that so Patricia would hug her, and it always worked. She acted like Patricia was a little girl, leaving for her first day of school. Donna liked having Patricia there in the evenings. She had someone to talk to and pass the time with when Charles was gone. Patricia gave Donna a long hug and headed out. Donna just went to the living room, sat on the couch, grabbed the remote, and turned on the television. It was pretty much like most of her days at home alone.

CHAPTER FOUR

****

Patricia rushed into her office cubicle because she was running a little behind. Strangely, she was good at helping Charles stay on time for work. However, that day she was late herself. She turned on her computer, but it did not work. She tried everything to get it to work, but she cannot. She signaled her boss, a sort of geeky Caucasian man in his thirties, to come over and check out the computer. "It's not working," Patricia said with a puzzled look on her face.

Her boss looked at her for a moment and said, "You won't be working here either if you come here late one more time." He tried to get Patricia's computer working, but he was unsuccessful. He picked up the phone and called for a Computer Technician. As her boss left, Patricia flipped him off behind his back. She started writing in her entries manually. About thirty minutes later, the Computer Technician, Andre Robinson, stuck his head in Patricia's cubicle. He sort of startled Patricia, and she jumped. "May I help you?" Patricia asked.

Andre held out his badge, which was hanging around his neck, and showed it to Patricia. "I am the computer technician. I was told your computer was down," Andre said as he stepped a little further into the cubicle. Patricia said, "Well, feel free to step on in." Patricia was drawn to Andre, and she couldn't take her eyes off him. In his first few minutes with Patricia, he had already been undressed and done some kinky things to her in her mind. Andre just stood there as if he were shy. Patricia gestured to Andre to come closer. When he did, she took his badge and looked at it more closely.

"Andre Robinson. That is a nice name. I like that," Patricia said in a flirtatious manner. Andre knew Patricia was coming on to him, but he wanted to keep it professional in the office. He was sort of feeling Patricia, too. Usually, Andre did not date women he met on his job, but perhaps he would make an exception this time. "Oh, I am sorry, my name is Patricia Campbell," Patricia said enthusiastically. Patricia just stood there for a minute, staring right at Andre. Andre cleared his throat to get Patricia's attention. "Well, let me get out of your way so you can do your job," Patricia said as she stepped aside. She did get his hint.

Even as she sat in her seat, she just could not take her eyes off Andre. She had not seen any man come into the office whom she was attracted to. Andre was the exception to the rule. Patricia was usually too busy to notice the other guys in her office or those who came in. Indeed, none of them made her feel this way. "I am going to go back to the break room now, so if you need anything, just ask someone here in the office for it," Patricia said as she headed out of her cubicle. "Is there some coffee back there?" Andre asked as he caught up to Patricia. Patricia said, "Hell yeah, they have coffee, and it is pretty damn good too."

Surprisingly, she preferred the coffee from her job to her mother's coffee. "I guess I could use a cup or two this morning," Andre said as he followed Patricia down the hall to the break room. Patricia was pouring Andre's coffee, but she was still staring at him. The coffee began to flow out of his cup and run down the counter. "Whoa!" Andre yelled as he jumped back. Patricia jumped as well when she up righted the coffee pot. Andre took some paper towels and started drying up the mess.

"Sorry about that, Andre," Patricia said as she grabbed some paper towels and assisted Andre. It was undoubtedly a good thing neither of them got burned. The only thing that was burned was Patricia's pride. She was truly embarrassed. "I am so sorry, Andre. I guess I'm a little clumsy this morning," Patricia said as she threw the used towels in the trash. One of the nosy females of the office, Charlotte, came into the break room. Charlotte was a Caucasian female in her thirties. She dressed like she was seventy.

Her fashions were out of date. Her shoes looked like she got her money's worth out of them back in the seventies. Andre and Patricia headed back to the office cubicle after Patricia signaled for them to leave the break room. Suddenly, they no longer needed coffee. Patricia's primary mission was to get out of there and away from Charlotte. Andre worked on the computer for only a few minutes. He turned on the computer to ensure all the systems worked properly. He said, "Patricia, your computer is as good as new," as he put his tools back in his bag.

"Wow, that was fast. How long have you been a computer geek? I mean technician," Patricia asked with a childish laugh. "About five years or so," Andre replied. Patricia said, "I have been working here for about two years and never had the opportunity to meet you." "That's because our contract with your company is fairly new. I think the other company went south of the border," Andre said as he looked at his watch and then at the exit. Andre needed to make his exit, so he looked at his watch again and said, "Patricia, I need to get going. It was certainly nice to meet you."

He reached into his pocket, gave Patricia one of his business cards, and said, "You can give me a call later on if you want, but now I need to roll." "Would I be calling for business or pleasure?" Patricia asked Andre with a seductive voice and a savvy smile. "Well, feel free to call me anytime. I am single, and I did not see a ring on your finger, so I assume you are not married." Patricia had trouble believing a man who looked like Andre could be single. She felt it was too good to be true. After all, it was not every day Patricia would meet a guy who at least seemed charming.

Andre did not seem to be like the thugs she had gotten accustomed to meeting. "If I call you, I am not going to get cussed out by some crazy bitch, right?" Patricia asked. "No, I promise you will not get cussed out by anyone. If you do, it will be by me, because that is my personal cell number. I am the only one that answers it," Andre joked.

Several days later, Patricia was getting ready for a date with Andre. Her parents looked at her strangely because Patricia was quite bubbly. "Okay, Patricia, tell us what's going on," Charles said. Patricia said, "Nothing is going on. I just happen to be in a good mood." Donna just looked at Patricia for a few seconds and said, "Patricia, just at least tell us his name for crying out loud."

You see, it was not the first time Patricia had that look about her. Donna knew that was the look of Patricia meeting someone. Patricia finally came clean and said, "I met a guy on my job a few days ago. He just seems so nice. And he is not a thug daddy!" Patricia would almost rather keep her relationship with Andre a secret. She knew her parents would eventually persuade her to let them meet him.

Patricia knew he would have to endure an intense evaluation and background check from Charles. Patricia wanted to avoid some of the questions about Andre, so she said. "I need to finish getting ready, so I will be back in a few." "What time should we expect you back tonight?" Donna asked. Patricia was unsure what Andre had planned and could not answer that question.

She was not even sure she would be coming home that night. She knew she would never hear the end of it if she stayed out all night. "At least tell us where he lives. He could be a damn ax murderer or serial killer for all we know. Hell, tell us something about this guy." Donna pleaded. Patricia said, "I will try to be home by about eleven or twelve. I will write some pertinent information about Andre before I leave."

She had to tread lightly with Charles because he was still protective of her and did not want her to date anyone. Besides, she was living in his home, so she had to walk a thin line. She felt she should abide by some of his rules if she wanted to stay there and keep the peace. A little while later, Patricia came out of her room with one of her nicest outfits. It certainly would not be considered her Sunday best.

Patricia probably would never wear a provocative outfit like that to church. She looked incredibly sexy with her hair and nails nicely done. Her shoes had at least four-inch heels. They were open-toed and revealed her well-manicured toes. Everything she had on matched up well. Her dress was form-fitting and a dark blue color. Patricia's primary mission was to thoroughly impress Andre. She knew this outfit would most likely do the job. "Where are you two planning to go tonight?" Donna asked as she wiped down the coffee table.

Patricia looked at Donna strangely at first, but then said, "I am not sure, but I think we will be going to dinner. I guess he wanted to keep it a secret." Charles gave Patricia a thorough head-to-toe evaluation. You could tell by his expression that he did not like her outfit. He did not need to say anything because both Donna and Patricia could read him quite well. He just went to the living room, fell into his favorite reclining seat, and turned on the television. He would most likely be up until Patricia came back home. He often felt Patricia was getting back at him for being so strict on her when she was a little girl.

The next day, Patricia and Andre walked into a charming and romantic restaurant. A Waitress, Tammy, led them to their table. The tables were all lit with candles, and flashing, colorful lights illuminated the place. A live band played soft jazz on a stage. Tammy, a young, attractive black woman in her twenties, seated Andre and Patricia and handed them both a menu. "Hello, my name is Tammy. I will be serving you this evening. Is there anything I can get you two started on?" Tammy asked. Patricia said, "Um, I guess I will have a Diet Seven Up." Andre said, "I will start with a nice glass of Merlot."

After Tammy left, Patricia felt it was time to ask Andre some more personal questions. She thought this would be a good time to open Andre up a little. "So, tell me something about yourself, Andre," Patricia said while adjusting her plate and silverware. Andre started to talk to Patricia, but he was abruptly interrupted by Tammy, who asked, "Are you folks ready to order?" Patricia glanced through the menu and said, "I will try your steak and lobster special, potato wedges, and a Caesar salad." Andre took his time looking through the menu.

Andre knew what he wanted already, but he was also checking out Tammy. That did not go unnoticed by Patricia. "I guess I will have the honey barbecued ribs, a baked potato, and Cole slaw," Andre said as he handed Tammy his menu. Tammy walked away after writing Patricia and Andre's orders. "Patricia, you have not said whether you like this place or not. I went out of my way to get this place for us," Andre said in a disappointed tone. Patricia looked around and said, "Oh, I think the restaurant is beautiful, and I appreciate the date."

Andre just did not seem to believe Patricia. He thought she might be telling him what he wanted to hear. So, he thought he would soften the mood by tricking her. "I am glad you like this place because we are going Dutch tonight," Andre said with a serious and convincing face. So convincing that Patricia believed him. She certainly was not prepared to pay anything for this night out on the town. She was expecting Andre to be a man and handle the date. "We're doing what?" Patricia asked. Andre laughed out loud and said, "I was just joking. Damn, you should have seen the expression on your face. You looked like a child getting his favorite toy taken away. Shoot, I would never do that on the first date.

Andre continued, saying, "Oh yeah, you want me to tell you something about myself. Well, I can tell you that my life might make a bestseller. I came from a broken home." Patricia said, "Oh, Andre, I am so sorry for prying. My intention was not to spoil the romantic mood." Andre said, "That's cool because I don't mind talking about my life." Andre believed he was completely over his traumatic childhood, so telling his story was somewhat therapeutic for him. He knew it was early in the relationship to share his story with her, but he felt comfortable with Patricia.

Tammy came back to their table, set their food down, and asked, "Is there anything else I can get you folks?" Patricia said, "I just want a glass of water." "I would like a refill on the Merlot," Andre said. When Tammy left, Andre started to have second thoughts about telling his story in the restaurant. He felt perhaps it was not the right time or place for him to tell his story. Andre put salt on his food and said, "You might be right about my story spoiling the mood. I don't think this is an appropriate place." Patricia was disappointed because she felt he was about to open to her.

Patricia's interest was aroused, and she was ready to hear Andre's story. Tammy came back and placed some dinner rolls, water, and the Merlot on the table. "Can I get you folks anything else?" Tammy asked cordially. Patricia was not feeling the repeated interruptions by Tammy. She thought Tammy was interrupting them on purpose, so she could flirt with Andre. Patricia was a bit insecure.

Even though Andre was not officially her man, she still felt like Tammy was being disrespectful. Every time she came to their table, she was smiling and checking out Andre. Patricia caught Andre checking Tammy out, too, even when she was not coming to their table. Tammy was beautiful, with a gorgeous figure, and that night she looked scantily clad. They were not at a Hooters restaurant, so Patricia wondered how Tammy got away with dressing that way. She looked a lot more tempting than Patricia did that night. "No, we are fine!" Patricia yelled. Tammy was startled and jumped. She looked at Patricia as if she were crazy and walked away rather quickly. Andre wondered what Patricia's problem was and said, "What the hell was that all about? Why did you yell at the waitress?"

"I wanted to hear more about you. The anticipation is killing me, and that heifer keeps coming over here disturbing us," Patricia answered. Andre decided to open and said, "I grew up watching my father abuse my mother. My father later abused me, too. My mother finally fled with me after she could not take it anymore. I have not seen my father in over twenty-five years."

Patricia was somewhat shocked that Andre would share his story with her. She would not be as willing to tell her story, which was very much like Andre's. "So, your mother raised you right?" Patricia asked. Andre said, "That is correct. My mother raised my older brother, me, and my younger sister. My older brother lives in Oregon, and my younger sister lives in Los Angeles." Patricia wiped her mouth with her napkin and asked, "Andre, how is your mother doing?" She was just being curious, and that seemed to be an appropriate question. Andre looked down for a second, looked at Patricia again, and said, "She died a year ago from a massive heart attack." "Oh, I apologize for your loss, and I hope you don't think I am prying too much." "No, I am okay. Telling my story is somewhat uplifting and empowering to me," Andre said.

Patricia sort of changed gears rather quickly and asked, "Have you ever been married?" Andre smiled, shook his head yes, and said, "Yeah, I have been married twice before." "You're only thirty-two, and you have been married two times? Well, what happened?" Patricia asked, once again prying. "I guess I was not ready for marriage those two times," Andre said. Patricia Jokingly said, "Andre, be honest; did you kill them?" Andre laughed and said, "Believe me, they are both alive and well."

Patricia drank a little water and asked, "Andre, do you have any kids?" Andre said, "I do not have any kids, so there isn't any baby mama drama going on here." Patricia bragged to Andre and said, "I don't have any kids either. No man, no kids, and no cat or dog." "So, tell me a little more about yourself, Patricia," Andre said. "Oh, Andre, maybe next time," Patricia quickly said. "Patricia, you know you are wrong for not telling me about yourself!" Patricia was feeling Andre, but she did not feel comfortable enough to open herself up to him just yet.

She cut her steak and said, "I promise you I will tell you more about myself next time." Andre asked, "Do you want to go downtown to that club called Club Spice? It is sort of like a thirty-plus club." Patricia said, "It is still pretty early, so what are we going to do after we eat?" Andre said, "Let's go check out that action flick called A Cop's Justice." "Is that the blockbuster action flick with Lucy Liu, Jet Li, Jackie Chan, and several other great martial artists?" Patricia asked. "Yeah, that's the one. Now, are you okay with an action flick? I mean, you are not just into those chick flicks, are you?"

Patricia giggled and said, "As long as there is lots of action in the movie, I will do an action movie. The only flicks I dislike are horror movies. They give me terrible nightmares." Andre took a quick bite out of one of his ribs and said, "I do not like the chick flicks. I'm okay with almost any other genre." Andre looked under the table and said, "It's a good thing you wore flat shoes tonight. I love to dance, and after the movie I plan to dance the night away with you. I am going to wear you out on the dance floor."

Patricia grinned and told Andre, "You are the one who is going to need medical attention, not me. I am warning you because I can get my dance on." Andre just laugh ed it off and did not believe Patricia. Later that evening, Patricia and Andre were on the dance floor of Club Spice. Flashing and blinking lights illuminated the dance floor. The dance floor was full of people doing the latest dances. Patricia was the better dancer and appeared to be wearing Andre out. Other people who were on the dance floor gathered around Patricia and Andre.

Andre, clearly outdone and embarrassed, grabbed Patricia's arm and led her back to the table. It was clear he was not a good loser. He took Patricia out to his car, and they both got in. Andre was exhausted. He rolled the car window down, put his seat in a reclining position, and said, "I should have known you would have all that damn energy." "Perhaps you should have thought before you started running your mouth about what you were going to do," Patricia said. Andre said, "It was the seven-year age difference between the two of us. If you were the same age, you would have been in trouble. Shoot, I used to be a great dancer at one time."

"Whatever! I had a good time, but I guess I'd better head back home," Patricia said. Andre readjusted his seat and said, "Okay, I will take you home. I wouldn't want your folks to send out a posse after us." The next morning, Patricia's co-worker, Charlotte, brought her a beautiful bouquet of long-stemmed red roses. There were balloons attached, and they floated freely above the bouquet. Patricia pulled off the little card that was attached. "I got a card too," Patricia said happily. Charlotte smiled and said, "Yeah, and the words are so sweet." Patricia's expression changed quickly to anger.

She could not believe Charlotte dared to read her card. She did not like Charlotte because she was always in everyone else's business. "How do you know what is in my card, Charlotte?" Patricia asked. Charlotte knew she had been caught at that point. She stood there for a few seconds with the "Deer in the headlights" look. Charlotte wanted to escape the embarrassing situation because the whole office was waiting for her to respond to Patricia.

Charlotte got up rather quickly, looked at the clock, and said, "Whoa, I better be getting back to work." "Yeah bitch, you need to get a life and stop messing around with folk's shit!" Patricia said as Charlotte left. Patricia read the card, and a big smile appeared on her face. She smelled the beautiful roses. The balloons read, "Just thinking of you."

CHAPTER FIVE

****

Later that week, Patricia was at home talking on the telephone. She was on the phone for quite a while. Patricia liked to talk on the landline phone because the reception was poor at her parents' house. Donna asked Patricia, "Can Charles and I use the phone sometimes?" Charles did not like Patricia being so involved with Andre at such an early point in their relationship. "You are spending an awful lot of time with this guy, Patricia. We hardly see you around here anymore," Charles said after Patricia hung up the phone.

Patricia said, "Andre is just such a nice guy." Charles replied, "They all seem nice at first." "You seemed nice at first, too," Donna joked. That was not too funny to Charles, but Donna and Patricia sure got a good laugh out of it. Later that afternoon, Andre and Patricia were on a ferry. They were taking in the beautiful scenery. Andre went behind Patricia and wrapped his arms around her waist. They both peered over the ferry's security rails as they enjoyed the view. Patricia was enjoying every moment, as she didn't get out often.

The wind blew through her hair like a modeling photo shoot. For the first time in a long time, Patricia felt a sense of specialness. Andre was truly showing his suave side, and Patricia loved it. Later that night, Patricia and Andre had a conversation in his car. The windows are notably steamed up. Andre started kissing Patricia rather passionately. He rubbed on her legs, and as his hand crept slowly up her dress. Patricia gently placed his hand in his lap. "So would you like to come over to my place for a while?" Andre asked Patricia.

Patricia said, "Andre, I do not feel that going to your place is such a good idea. And I say that more for myself. I know how I am feeling about you now." "But, shit, we have been seeing each other for nearly two weeks, and you have never come by my house!" "Maybe another time," Patricia said while rolling down her window for air. Andre pretty much knew his chances were slim to get Patricia over to his place, but he planned to keep trying. "Why do you always ask me when it's late at night? I don't want to be just your booty call," Patricia told Andre. Andre just started the car and took off. He was disappointed and felt somewhat rejected.

However, Andre was still not ready to give up on Patricia so easily. He looked over to Patricia with his little boy's innocent look and asked, "You sure you don't just want to stop by for a minute?" Patricia said, "Okay, we can drive over there so I can see your place, but I will not go inside this time." Andre knew that if she were willing to go all the way over to his house, he would easily convince her to go inside.

A little while later, Patricia did make it over to Andre's place. However, they still had not made it out of the car. The two of them were making out so intensely that they appeared to be wrestling. They both began to practically tear each other's clothes off. "Andre, hold on a second. Do you have one of those things?" Patricia asked while still breathing heavily. Andre started fishing around and fumbling through his car for a condom. His pants were almost down to his thighs. He hoped he had at least one condom in there, or this passionate evening would surely end abruptly. He opened his junky glove compartment, moved a few things around, and pulled out a whole box of condoms.

Patricia was surprised that he would be so sexually prepared, but she did not want to say anything that would spoil the moment. "Okay, baby, I will go inside with you. Just for a little while," Patricia said submissively. Patricia was good and ready to have Andre right then and there. She could see that Andre was ready, too. Nevertheless, she did not feel like having sex in the car. She figured, why do it in the cramped vehicle when she was sure it would be more comfortable in his bed? Besides, they were right in front of his house.

Andre was so excited that he was about to leave the condoms in the car and jump out of the car with his pants still down. "Baby, you are forgetting something," Patricia reminded Andre. Andre quickly pulled his pants up, fastened them, and grabbed the condoms as they exited the car. At that point, there was no doubt about what was going to take place. Patricia and Andre both knew what was getting ready to happen. Neither of them was going to stop this moment from happening. They got to the front door, but because Andre was so excited, he fumbled with the keys for a little while.

Patricia sighed and stood there patiently; her arms crossed over her chest. Andre briefly paused, looked up at her, and began to laugh. It appeared Patricia was sporting the Don King look. Her hair was all over the place. She asked, "Why are you laughing?" Andre refused to answer her. He may as well have pleaded the fifth. They finally did make it inside after Andre tried his fourth or fifth key. They busted through the front door, and Andre led Patricia right back to his bedroom as if he were on a mission.

Andre's house was big for a bachelor pad. There was a long hall that led back to the rooms. He had beautiful pictures hanging on the walls. He carried Patricia through the house and gently placed her in his king-sized bed. Andre made wild, passionate love to Patricia for quite a while. They went at it two more times. Andre trembled wildly, made several faces, and collapsed on top of Patricia for the third and last time. Patricia just gently laid Andre down next to her. Andre was clearly out of gas. After all, he had made love to Patricia three times in a row, and each time was for an extended period. Andre just lies in the bed next to Patricia, knocked out and sleeping like a newborn.

Patricia was well satisfied. She lay there shaking uncontrollably. She fell fast asleep shortly after Andre. The next morning, Andre tossed and turned wildly as he had another one of his nightmares about his childhood. Patricia shook Andre, waking him up. He jumped up and practically pushed Patricia out of the bed. He looked combative as he stood there in a fighting stance. "Andre, it's me. I think you were having a bad nightmare," She quickly reminded him.

Andre sat on the edge of the bed to get his bearings and shake out the cobwebs. "It's okay, I deal with these damn nightmares all the time," Andre said. Andre looked over at his alarm clock and jumped up suddenly to get ready for work. "Oh damn, I am going to be late for work," he said. "Today is Sunday, you are off," Patricia told Andre. Andre just shook his head and sat back down on the bed. "Andre, are you hungry?" Andre said, "Yeah, I am starving!" "Do you want to go out to breakfast? There must be a waffle or pancake house near here," Patricia hinted as she lay back on the pillows. Andre looked at her like she cussed at him and said, "Why go to breakfast when I can cook breakfast for us? I promise you I can make a nice breakfast."

Andre went to the closet, got a robe for Patricia, and asked, "Are you okay with us taking a shower together? Hey, I am into the water conservation thing." Patricia was not comfortable enough to let Andre see her naked in broad daylight. She had not come from under the covers yet. However, she thought it was Andre's way of keeping things on a romantic level. She felt that at that point, it didn't matter anyway.

Patricia quickly put on the robe while she was still under the covers and said, "Sounds good to me, but let me use your phone to call my folks to let them know I am okay. I forgot to plug my cell phone in last night, so the battery is dead." Andre did not like Patricia calling her folks so often when they were together. Patricia sometimes called them more than once when she and Andre were together. "Damn girl, you are calling them again?" Andre asked with an attitude. "Why do you get an attitude every time I call my parents?" "Girl, you are spoiling the mood." Patricia sat on the edge of the bed. She needed to talk about this with Andre. "Well, you are not a damn sixteen-year-old, but you are constantly calling your folks when we are out," Andre said.

"Maybe that's because my parents, especially my dad, worry about me. Besides, they have not even met you, but you had me out all night." "That is bullshit because your parents do not need to know your every move!" "Why are we even arguing about this? It is not a subject for discussion. Now, can I use your phone or not?" Patricia asked. Andre took the phone and sort of tossed it to Patricia. He was distraught at that point. "Here is the Goddamn phone!" Andre said. "What is your problem, Andre?" "Patricia, you are the one with the problem!"

Patricia slammed the phone down and got up to leave. She began gathering her belongings and getting dressed simultaneously. She was so angry that she could have walked nearly twenty miles to her parents' house. Andre just stood in front of the door to block Patricia's departure. Patricia calmly asked Andre, "Would you just please move so I can leave?" Patricia attempted to get by Andre but was unsuccessful. When she finally nearly did get by, Andre grabbed her by her arm. Patricia snatched her arm from Andre and yelled, "Let me go, Andre!"

Andre said, "I'm sorry, baby, I just had a terrible nightmare." "Don't talk to me like that! I am not some slut from the hood," Patricia told Andre. The mood was undoubtedly spoiled now because she was hurt. Patricia once again started to push by Andre and said, "Just take me home, Andre." They paused momentarily, as if to catch their breath. Andre put his arms around Patricia and pulled her close to him. Patricia tried to resist him just for a moment. She gave in and wrapped her arms around him.

They sat on the bed and held each other. Patricia still wanted some answers and said, "Gee, what was that all about? I mean, last night was so beautiful, and then we woke up ready to kill each other." "I guess I am starting to fall for you. So, maybe I am a little afraid," Andre replied as he held Patricia a little closer and tighter. Patricia was flattered, but she wanted to know what he was so afraid of. Before she could ask him, he said, "Everyone I get close to either leaves me or dies." "It is not your fault, Andre. You cannot change things that happened to you in the past. At some point, you will have to try to get on with your life."

Andre did not like Patricia lecturing him on life, so he quickly changed the subject. "So, how about that breakfast? Are you still hungry?" Andre asked. Patricia, now calm, said, "Andre, I am starving and I'm about ready for that nice breakfast you promised." Even though she didn't think he was terrific in the kitchen, she still appreciated his efforts. She remembered how he told her he was on the dance floor. Perhaps this time he was doing the same thing.

So far, she noticed that when he bragged about something, he usually sucked at it. That certainly held true with the sex. Andre had never bragged about how good he was in bed, yet she felt thoroughly satisfied by him. Andre fooled Patricia this time. He had prepared a nice breakfast for her. The breakfast included an omelet, pancakes, toast, sausage, sliced melon, and orange juice. Patricia was feeling outstanding because she found a man who knew his way around a kitchen. She thought he pretty much knew his way around a bedroom, too. As Patricia sat at the table to enjoy the meal, she said, "Honey, I am sort of feeling you, too." She just wanted to wait until the right time to tell him. Since Andre expressed his feelings for her, she felt the time was right.

A week later, Patricia, Yvette, and Vanessa were at the beach on a beautiful summer day. Children ran around laughing, swimming, and playing as their parents kept a watchful eye on them. The girls all had beach chairs, and a large umbrella shaded them from the sun. Patricia said, "I like Andre. He seems different from the other guys I have dated." Vanessa and Yvette were surely not taking her seriously. They believed she was more in lust than anything else. Indeed, they felt she had not had any good love in a while. "Shit, you're worse than Yvette, and you are not even married," Vanessa said.

Yvette adjusted the rather large beach umbrella and said, "Oh, tying the knot is probably next for that girl. She practically lives with him now." Patricia said, "No matter what happens, the three of us will always be tight." Sure, it sounded pretty good because Yvette's marriage to Roger never stopped their friendship from being tight. Vanessa asked, "Why haven't you allowed me and Yvette to meet Andre?" Usually, Patricia was so excited about having a man that she could not wait to show him off. She knew Yvette and Vanessa were brutally honest, and she thought they would be critical of Andre.

Patricia rubbed some lotion on her legs and said, "I promise you two will meet Andre soon. Believe me, I think both of you will be impressed. This one is not a thug." Vanessa asked, "Patricia, why does Andre call you and make you come home almost every time we're out? It's like he does not want you with us." "It's not like that. He just likes to spend a lot of time with me," Patricia said as she tried to defend Andre's actions. Three well-built African American gentlemen approach the girls. They were wearing swim trunks and stood over the girls, as if waiting for an invitation.

Sean was a tall, dark-skinned man in his early thirties. He had a bald head, a goatee, and was well-built. Robert was the shortest of the three. He was a light-skinned black man, about twenty-five years old. His eyes were hazel, and he was also well-built. Barry was close to Sean's size, about six feet. He was a little lighter than Sean and about thirty years old. He was not as well-built as Sean and Robert. "Hello, ladies. My name is Sean, and these are my two friends, Robert and Barry. How are you, fine ladies, doing on this beautiful day?" Vanessa stood up, shook Sean's hand, and said, "I am Vanessa, and these are my two best friends, Patricia and Yvette."

Vanessa held on to Sean's hand for a few more seconds as she sort of gave him her head-to-toe evaluation. She was notably impressed. Robert asked, "Is it okay if we join you?" Vanessa was quick to say, "Sure, you guys can have a seat with us if you like." Yvette slapped Vanessa on the thigh because she felt Vanessa was being fast and acting desperate. Vanessa just held her hand up to Yvette, as if to remind her that she was not married and could do whatever she wanted. I suppose we should have asked if you ladies are taken. Not that it matters nowadays," Sean said as he slid a little closer to Vanessa.

Yvette proudly and loudly said, "Well, I am happily married, and it matters to me." Barry asked, "Is anyone else either married or otherwise spoken for?" Patricia was only able to get the words "Well, I am…" before Vanessa cut her off. "She's spoken for, too! She isn't married, but she might as well be," Vanessa said. Patricia kicked Vanessa to let her know she needed to shut up and mind her own business. Andre had followed Patricia and was watching her from the beach boardwalk. He had even brought some binoculars. Andre was upset about Patricia's relationship with her two girlfriends.

Andre believed they were influencing Patricia, and he was somewhat jealous of their closeness. Andre yelled out, "Those two bitches!" There were other people near Andre when he had his outburst, including a woman, her young daughter, and son. The woman stepped back, looked at Andre, and walked off rather quickly with her son and daughter, nearly dragging them. Andre was so angry that he was oblivious to his negative behavior.

He pulled out his cell phone and dialed Patricia's number. He watched and waited as Patricia ignored her ringing cell phone. She even looked at her phone and then put it back in her bag. Andre shook his head and stormed away. He would surely have a bone to pick with Patricia when she got home. "I guess I am going to have to straighten her ass out about those two whores!" Andre said to himself as he stormed away.

CHAPTER SIX

****

It is about six months later. Patricia is at her parents' home with Vanessa and Yvette. Patricia's parents are away on vacation. She poured some champagne into Vanessa's glass. Usually, when the girls drank champagne, they were celebrating something. Therefore, Yvette and Vanessa knew something was up. Patricia leaned across the table and used her left hand to balance herself as she poured the champagne. Her very noticeable engagement ring was now visible.

"Damn girl, what did you do to him? You must have rocked his world! I mean, just look at that rock on your finger," Vanessa said. Yvette picked up Patricia's hand to get a closer look at the ring and said, "Patricia, you didn't!" Patricia said, "Andre just proposed to me yesterday and I said hell yeah!" Yvette and Vanessa were both baffled by this. They both looked at each other in utter disbelief. Vanessa picked up Patricia's hand to also get a closer look at the ring and said, "Girl, you have only known that boy for about three or four months."

Patricia took offence to Vanessa's statement and said, "It has been six months, miss know-it-all, and my man is not a boy!" Yvette said, "Vanessa is just tripping as usual. Her man is the one who is the boy." Yvette did not want Vanessa to be too harsh or overshadow Patricia. Vanessa always spoke her mind, but sometimes it was detrimental to her. Yvette said, "Vanessa, none of your boyfriends have been worth a shit, and they all have been like immature boys."

Patricia knew their conversation was leading to an argument. She placed a bowl of potato chips on the table and said, "Look, I just wanted to hear some good marriage advice. I mean, not that any of your advice will change my mind." Vanessa said, "Well, sister, I have never been married, so Yvette is the one who should respond to anything dealing with marriage." For once, Patricia agreed with Vanessa. At least this time, her advice was good, so she turned to hear from Yvette. Yvette said, "Patricia, there are no big secrets to a successful relationship or marriage. My marriage with Roger lasts because there is love, understanding, trust, and respect." "Uh-oh, looks like we got Doctor Ruth started," Vanessa said. Yvette and Patricia said simultaneously, "Vanessa, shut up!"

Patricia took a sip of champagne and said, "I think I have that type of relationship with Andre." Vanessa, once again being negative, said, "How the hell do you know that after only six months? Girl, you probably don't even know his shoe size!" "His shoe size is ten and a half, smart-ass!" Patricia blurted out. Vanessa said, "Wow! So is the shoe size thing true?" Patricia grinned and said, "None of your business. It's for me to know and you to find out. But your fast needs to find out from another brother!" Patricia was not going to volunteer too much more information to Vanessa. She knew it would only be giving her ammunition.

Yvette grabbed a handful of chips and asked, "Are we ever going to get a chance to meet Andre?" Patricia did bottoms up with her champagne and said, "I promise you will get to meet him soon." She took out a photo of Andre, showed it to Yvette, and said, "Meantime, I will let you see a photo of my baby." "This is him? Damn, he is fine," Yvette said. Vanessa snatched the picture and said, "Yeah, he is fine. Does he have a brother?" Patricia snatched the picture back and said, "Andre does have a brother, but he would not want your ass! Besides, he lives way out-of-state in Oregon."

Yvette said, "Andre's brother is only a short flight from here. So, you should go for it, girl." Vanessa leaned back in her seat and said, "Now you know damn well I don't do the long-distance thing. And you know I do not do the friendly skies thing." She had only flown one time in her life and vowed never to do it again. Most of Vanessa's boyfriends lived within a twenty-five- to fifty-mile radius of her home. Yvette asked, "What did your mother and father say about you getting hitched?" "They both think I lost it, but they will get to finally meet him on Friday," Patricia said.

Vanessa said, "Shit, I would love to be a fly on the wall when your parents meet Andre. Lord knows your father is going to act like a fool." Patricia knew her parents, especially her father, would never accept the fact that she was grown. To them, she would always be their little girl. After all, she was their only child. Vanessa laughed and said, "Shit, my parents were glad to see me get out of the house. I think they had a huge party when I left." Patricia and Yvette thought that was funny. They could see how her parents would be happy to see her leave.

"So, have you two set a date yet?" Yvette asked. "We don't have an official date yet, but I am pretty sure it will not be too far in the future," Patricia said happily. "Well, I guess congratulations and a toast are in order," Yvette said. As they clicked their glasses together, Yvette said, "To a prosperous marriage." "Yeah, congratulations, girlfriend, now a real celebration is in order. So, I just want to know where the party is going to be." Vanessa said. She would be there for any celebration or party.

She never missed any parties or celebrations of any kind with the girls and was usually the life of the party. Patricia said, "Well, I guess it looks like we will be doing Club Spice on Friday. It is going to be ladies' night, and they will have plenty of strippers there. I reserved the back portion for us and our male dancer. Since it is our night out, I went all out and got Big Chocolate Papa. I am sure he is going to show us what he's working with." Patricia turned on the radio, and the girls started doing their dance routines. It started looking like a party was about to get underway right there at the house.

Friday finally arrived. This was the day Patricia's parents would get to meet Andre. Charles and Donna patiently awaited Andre's arrival. Charles read the newspaper, and Donna prepared the meal. It was her famous spaghetti. As it got later, Charles began to worry. Charles looked at his watch and said, "Honey, I don't think they're going to show." Donna was not so impatient and believed they were just running late. It was not like Patricia to say she was going to do something like this and not follow through with it.

She calmed Charles down by saying, "They are probably stuck in traffic. I am sure they will be coming through the door any second now." Almost on cue, the front door opened, and in came Patricia and Andre. Andre was well dressed in a pair of nice slacks and a shirt. He was also well-groomed. Patricia looked sexy, too. The four of them just stood there looking at each other. Patricia finally spoke and said, "Oh, I am sorry, Andre, this is my mother, Donna, and my father, Charles. Mom and Dad, this is Andre." Even after Andre had been officially introduced, they still stood there staring at each other.

Donna finally broke the silence and said, "Oh, excuse my manners, Andre, you two come on in and have a seat. It's great to finally meet you. We have heard so much about you." Andre smiled and said, "Well, I hope it was all good." Andre was very good at winning people over. He was a knowledgeable individual and an excellent communicator. He could be funny at times when he wanted. These were some of the very characteristics that won over Patricia. Nevertheless, Patricia still felt that Andre's personality and bright smile would not win over her father.

"So, you plan on marrying my daughter, right?" Charles asked with a serious, stone-faced look. Andre answered confidently saying, "Yes, sir, that is the plan." Charles asked, "Andre, how old are you?" "I am thirty-two, sir." Charles asked, "Andre, are you ex-military?" Andre looked at Patricia, then back to her father and said, "No, sir, I have never been in the military, why?" "I was just curious because you keep on calling me sir. Feel free to call me Charles." Andre was starting to realize Charles did not particularly like him marrying his daughter. He could tell that by the way Charles asked the questions.

Andre wanted to take some of the punch out of Charles' questions and show Patricia he could stand up to her father. "Look, I am sure you have a lot of questions for me, so feel free to ask me anything," Andre said. Donna jumped right in and asked, "Have you ever been married?" She and Charles nearly fell out of their seats when Andre replied, "Yes, I have been married twice before." Charles asked, "What happened with the other two marriages?" "Well, I guess I was not ready for marriage those times, but I am ready now, Andre replied."

Charles was still recovering from Andre's response to Donna's question when he asked, "So what do you do for a living?" "I work on computers. I am a computer Technician." Donna's eyes lit up like a child on Christmas morning. She felt Patricia had a man who was achieving great things and earning a good income. Charles wanted to know as much as possible about Andre because Patricia always seemed to attract men who were no good for her. "What about your family, young man?" Charles asked. Andre said, "I have an older brother in Oregon and a younger sister in Southern California. I get to see them from time to time." Charles asked, "What about your parents?"

You could practically hear a pin drop. Patricia just looked at Charles and shook her head. She knew her father would eventually find a chink in Andre's armor. As Donna saw Patricia and Andre's reaction, she knew something was not right with that question. "I have not seen my father for many years. He abused my mother, my brother, my sister, and me. My mother fled with us when we were all still young." Andre paused for a few seconds and said, "My mother just died of a massive heart attack last year." Donna quickly said, "Andre, we certainly apologize for opening old wounds."

Charles did not seem too sorry, as he was trying to figure out what made Andre tick. Moreover, that was the only way he could get to know him. Patricia took Andre's hand and stood up with him in preparation to leave. "Andre, we'd better get going. It is getting kind of late," Patricia said as she looked at her watch. The fact is, she wanted to get Andre out of there as quickly as possible. She felt she needed to rescue Andre from Charles. Donna thought she needed to make things right with Andre. She felt somewhat sorry for him. She knew the way to most men's hearts is through their stomachs.

Donna had also taken the time to prepare dinner for them and did not want Andre to leave without trying her cooking. Donna stood up and said, "You all are not going to stay? I cooked some of my famous spaghetti." Charles laughed and took a poke at Donna's famous spaghetti by saying, "Oh boy, and the old famous spaghetti! You two better get going while the getting is good." "That's okay, honey. You will be having soup and crackers tonight. Looks like you will be going on my famous quick weight loss plan," Donna said jokingly, but with a serious face.

Andre shook Charles' hand, and Donna hugged Andre and Patricia. Once again, Charles gave Andre a stare down for a few seconds. If looks could kill, Andre would have surely been a fatality. Charles grabbed hold of Andre's hand once again with a substantial grip. "So, I take it we will be seeing you again real soon," Charles said. Andre grimaced notably and said, "Yeah, I will be seeing you again real soon." Charles finally let Andre's hand go. Andre shook the feeling back into his hand while still grimacing. Charles was trying to convey a message to Andre, and Andre was feeling it quite clearly.

As Andre and Patricia got ready to walk out of the house, Andre stopped and turned around. "By the way, it was nice meeting you two," Andre said as he and Patricia left. "I can't pinpoint it, but there is something funny about him. I can just feel that there's something not right with him." Charles said after he closed the door and locked it. Donna believed Andre was a lovely young man and said, "Oh, honey, you never liked any of Patricia's boyfriends!" Charles said, "Obviously, I have never been wrong because Patricia is not with any of those thugs now."

Donna headed to the kitchen and said, "Oh, honey, please! I am going to finish dinner. Have you ever thought that maybe you ran some of the good ones away? Remember Jeff and Tyrone? They were not thugs." "I am going to say it one more time. There is something wrong with Andre. Once again, you will be saying I told you so," Charles responded. Donna was not going to listen to Charles' negative comments. Andre had answered all her questions as well as his.

Donna was delighted with Andre and felt he was good for Patricia. Surely, she felt any man who could stand up to Charles' military-like interrogation was probably okay. Then again, Patricia did get Andre out of there before Charles could lean into him.

CHAPTER SEVEN

****

It was now about three months from the infamous meeting. Andre, Patricia, Donna, Charles, Yvette, Vanessa, and other friends and family are present. They were all gathered to witness Patricia and Andre's wedding. This was an outdoor wedding featuring numerous flowers and elaborate decorations. It was a beautiful day, and about thirty to forty guests were seated on the lawn in chairs. The guests were mainly made up of Patricia's family and friends. Andre just had a couple of black male friends present. His brother and sister were not present.

Patricia and Andre looked like a fairy tale couple as they rode away in a horse-driven carriage. Donna could hardly get hold of herself, and the tears continuously streamed down her face. Her little girl has grown up and is now married. Charles' expression looked very similar to the one he had when he met Andre. Even at the wedding, where he should have been happy, he seemed upset. At this point, Charles still had not accepted Andre. He just knew Patricia could do better.

Perhaps he had hoped her "Mr. Right" would be a doctor or lawyer. Patricia was thrilled. This was the day she waited for, and she was glowing like a firefly the whole time. She did not shed one tear. Andre was the one who became overwhelmed with emotion. He tried unsuccessfully to choke back his tears. Yvette cried like a baby the whole wedding. Maybe it was because she was married and could fully identify with the situation. Vanessa did not cry at all. She was always the toughest one in the group. Neither Yvette nor Patricia had ever seen Vanessa cry.

They had known each other for all those years, yet they had never seen Vanessa cry. Even when she stepped on a nail that was sticking through a board, she did not cry. Vanessa was about seven years old when the incident happened. She just grabbed the board and pulled it, along with the nail, out of her foot. She barely grimaced. She was a regular "GI Jane." Several weeks later, Patricia had come home from work early. She sat down on the couch to relax and turned on the television. It was the first time in a very long time that Patricia had any time off after work. She wanted to take full advantage of it. She fell asleep on the couch.

Later that evening, Andre came home from work. He just stood there staring at Patricia for a little while. He slammed the door, causing Patricia to jump up. "What the hell are you doing?" Andre asked. Patricia tried to get her bearings and said, "What do you mean? I got home early, so I am relaxing." Andre was angry. He walked up and turned the television off. Once again, he stopped and looked at Patricia with a scary, mean look and said, "You can relax after you fix my damn dinner!"

Patricia was in a state of shock. She could not understand why Andre was talking to her like that. Surely, she was entitled to some relaxation time. She did not want to make him any angrier, but she asked, "Why are you talking to me like that?" "If you don't get your big ass in there and cook my dinner, you are going to wish you had!" Patricia started a sentence and said, "But Andre, I was going to…" He cut her off and said, "Patricia, you are my wife now, and as my wife, you are going to do whatever I say. Now, that is just the way it is going to be." He walked up to the couch and got right in Patricia's face.

Pointing in her face, he said, "I let you run your big ass mouth long enough, and I put up with your little funky attitude long enough too. Now go cook my dinner before you piss me off." Patricia wisely went into the kitchen and did what she was told. She shakes her head and wonders if this is a preview of things to come as far as Andre is concerned. She was hoping it was just an isolated incident that stemmed from him having a terrible day at work. She had seen him mad before, and they even had argued before like couples sometimes do, but never like this. Patricia felt terrible.

She tore off some paper towels to wipe her tears as she prepared the meal. Andre pretty much took Patricia's spot on the couch, grabbed the remote, and started channel surfing like nothing ever happened. Later that evening, Patricia ate dinner with Andre. After Andre had eaten, he had several beers. Patricia saw that Andre had calmed down and relaxed. Patricia said, "Andre, I am going to Vanessa's house for a little while." Andre just looked at Patricia with a mean look, looked at his watch, and said, "Fine, but you better have your ass back here in two hours! Please don't make me have to come looking for you." I don't like that bitch anyway!"

Patricia arrived at Vanessa's house about twenty minutes later. Vanessa lived in a somewhat small apartment. It was cozy for her, and she liked the tranquility of living alone. Yvette was already there, and she let Patricia in. Yvette and Patricia went into the living room and sat on the couch. Yvette and Vanessa knew something was up because Patricia called the little meeting from her cell phone on the way there. Vanessa came into the living room shortly thereafter and had a seat. "So, what is it that you wanted to tell us?" Vanessa asked.

Patricia lowered her head sadly and said, "Andre went off on me earlier tonight." Yvette asked, "Did Andre hit you?" Patricia said, "He did not hit me, but I sure thought he would. For the first time, I felt terrified of Andre. It was like he was someone else." Vanessa said, "Oh, girl, you have not even been married a full month yet! You interrupted my dinner for that?" "Now tell us exactly what happened, Patricia," said Yvette. Patricia said, "Well, he yelled at me, threatened me, and cussed me out because his dinner was not ready when he got home. I had just gotten off work and I was beat."

Vanessa shook her head and said, "I bet Andre is one of those men who expect you to wait on them hand and foot and hold down a full-time job too." "Shit! I am not a damn robot. I was tired as hell myself when I got home from work," Patricia said emphatically. Vanessa turned down the television with the remote and asked Patricia, "Girl, you didn't see this coming?" Patricia said, "I mean, we had little meaningless arguments before, but I never saw him act like that. I have never seen that type of rage in Andre's eyes." Patricia forgot about the first time they made love at his house. Andre was mean then, too.

Patricia continued and said, "He told me now that we are married, things are going to change, and that he is the man of the house, so what he says goes." Yvette wanted to insert her opinion as usual. She tried to give Patricia the scoop about being married and help her through the situation. Yvette said, "It is perfectly normal for couples to argue sometimes, but they should never disrespect each other. Calling each other out of your names is also off-limits. Then there is that important ingredient called communication. I expect you to be able to talk to Andre normally, just like we're talking right now. I want you to discuss the argument with Andre once he cools off."

Vanessa jumped up and said, "I knew that fool was no good!" "Vanessa! Why do you always have to say some negative bullshit?" Yvette asked. Vanessa headed to the kitchen and said, "You two have too much drama in your lives for me!" She just fanned them off and left the room. It was times like these that made Vanessa glad she was single. She always listened when Yvette's marriage was new, and she was going through problems with her husband. Now, Vanessa had to hear about Patricia's issues with her new marriage.

It is now the next evening after the incident with Andre. Patricia was preparing Andre's dinner. She was still in her work clothes. She was notably exhausted as she rushed around the kitchen to put the finishing touches on the meal. Andre walked in the door and looked around. The house was cleaned up very nicely. Several candles were lit throughout the home. Andre sat on the couch and turned the television on to the evening news. He never even kissed or embraced Patricia after his long, hard day of work. Patricia was trying to set the tone by incorporating one of Yvette's key relationship ingredients.

Patricia planned to simply try to communicate with Andre. She hoped he was in a better mood. She tried to do everything right for him so he wouldn't have any reason to become upset with her. Patricia wiped the sweat off her forehead and said, "Hello, honey, dinner is ready. How was your day?" Andre gestured to Patricia and said, "Bring my food in here." Patricia brought Andre's food to him on a tray. She then sat next to him and asked, "Are you sure you want to eat in the living room? I have the dining room set up for the two of us." She had worked way too hard setting up the occasion and wanted things to go as planned.

Andre started gulping down his food like a wild animal and ignored Patricia. He turned up the television a little louder. Patricia stares at him for a while, anticipating his answer. This surely could not be what Yvette meant about communication. "I am fine in here," Andre said with his mouth full of food. "Andre, I wanted to talk to you. Baby, can you at least turn the television down?" Andre turned the television down slightly. She said, "I wanted the two of us to eat in the dining room together." She did not feel comfortable trying to talk to Andre with the television on.

Andre still had the television quite loud. "What do you want to talk about? Can't you see I just got home, and I am not in the mood to talk?" Andre asked with a frustrated tone. Patricia started to get a little nervous. Andre did not seem to be as cool as she had hoped. Even though she was anxious and somewhat scared, she was determined to talk to Andre this night. "Honey, I just wanted to talk with you about the argument we had last night," Patricia said with a very soft, convincing voice. "Well, talk!" Andre shouted. "Andre, I felt the way you spoke to me last night was wrong."

She hoped he would apologize so the two of them could get past the whole ordeal. Andre went off on Patricia and said, "Is that how you feel? I think you are just listening to your bitch ass girlfriends and your damn parents." Patricia got upset and said, "Please do not talk about my family or my two best friends." Strangely enough, he could call Patricia any name he wanted, but not her family or friends. She would not tolerate that. "Will you please just shut the hell up before you spoil my appetite?" Andre shouted. The previous evening was fresh on Patricia's mind, and she felt this discussion was heading in that direction like an out-of-control locomotive.

Patricia was momentarily speechless and had no idea what to say next. "But honey, I thought we could discuss what happened last night over dinner," Patricia said in a soft voice. "There is nothing to discuss! You will have my dinner ready for me when I come home every damn night. No ifs ands or buts! I want you to put in your two-week notice for your job tomorrow," Andre said as he bit off a huge chunk of chicken leg like a caveman. Andre continued, saying, "Patricia, I make enough money, so you do not need to work." "Baby, I would not feel right about that. I like my job. Besides, two salaries will always be better than one," Patricia said, with a pleading voice.

Andre was growing increasingly annoyed with Patricia. Patricia looked at Andre like she was going to talk again, but Andre put up the "talk to the hand" sign to shut Patricia up. He was warning her that he had heard enough, and she had better stop while she was ahead. Patricia started talking anyway and said, "Andre, I just don't think that you're being fair. I should be able to have a say in a decision like this."

Andre threw his plate of food towards her and said, "Are you satisfied? You spoiled my whole damn evening and managed to piss me off all in a matter of minutes. Now, clean that shit up and get me another plate of food!" Patricia just stood there for a minute, basically in shock. It was as if she were frozen in place. Andre pointed towards the kitchen and said, "Move your big ass!" Patricia brought Andre another plate of food. She went back in the kitchen and returned with a rag, broom, and dustpan to clean up Andre's mess. "You better wipe that look off your ugly face, bitch!"

"Andre, I should not have to put up with this kind of treatment. I have done nothing wrong." "Patricia, shut up because I am already pissed off." Patricia attempted to storm away with an attitude. She had put up with all she could and did not plan on taking any more. "Fine!" Patricia shouted. Andre jumped up off the couch, grabbed Patricia by the arm, and said, "I told you I am not going to put up with your crap anymore!" "Andre, you are hurting me," Patricia yelled. Andre slapped Patricia across the face and said, "See what you made me do? I told you to shut up."

Patricia sat down on the couch and began to cry as she held her eye. With that slap, Andre marked the beginning of the physical abuse. Oh, he had grabbed her by the arm before, but he had never struck her. Andre watched her for a minute and then shook his head. He was feeling somewhat remorseful at that point. He sighed and sat next to Patricia to console her. Andre rubbed Patricia's back for a minute and said, "I am sorry, baby. I didn't mean for that to happen. I just had a bad day at work today. My boss was on my ass all day."

Patricia said, "Baby, what is happening to us? I feel like we're growing apart and that all we do is fight now." Andre started running his hand through Patricia's hair and said, "Nothing is the matter with us or the relationship. We still love each other, right?" "Andre, you just struck me." "Baby, I am sorry, and I promise you it will never happen again. Look, baby, you know I love you. You know I would never do anything to intentionally hurt you, and you know that was not me a few minutes ago." Patricia replied, "I am willing to let it go as long as it will not happen again. Honey, we need to try to get along better." Andre hugged Patricia and said, "Everything is going to be all right."

Andre moved Patricia's hand from her face so he could view the damage he had caused. He gave her a black eye. He went into the kitchen and returned with an ice pack, handing it to Patricia. Andre tried to downplay Patricia's bruise by saying, "Patricia, your eye is not too bad. I assure you; the whole incident was just a terrible mistake that will never happen again. I still insist you give notice at your job." Patricia reluctantly said, "Okay, Andre, I will put in my two-week notice tomorrow." At this point, she would do anything to keep Andre at peace.

CHAPTER EIGHT

****

Yvette and Vanessa were over at Patricia's house this time. Patricia wanted Andre to meet Yvette and Vanessa so he would realize they were good people. Perhaps he would see why they are her best friends. Yvette and Patricia played Scrabble while Patricia quickly prepared Andre's food. She knows Andre will be home soon, but she takes the opportunity to sit down with the girls for a while. She was wearing shades in the house, which Yvette and Vanessa thought was strange.

They quickly figured out what was going on, but they wanted to wait for Patricia to talk about it. Patricia finally did take her glasses off, revealing her black eye. Yvette could no longer sit there quietly. She said, "Girl, what happened to your eye?" Patricia paused for a second to make something up. She said, "I fell down the porch stairs." Vanessa asked, "How the hell did you manage to fall on your face?" Patricia became annoyed and said, "I just happened to trip, so can we move on to another topic?" Yvette said, "No way, girl! We are not going to go to another topic."

Yvette and Vanessa knew what the deal was, but they wanted Patricia to be honest with them and tell them what happened. Yvette said, "Patricia, we all go back a long way, so you know Vanessa and I were not born yesterday." "Andre did that, didn't he?" Vanessa asked. Patricia once again paused and said, "Yeah, he got a little upset and hit me. Now you know, so are you two satisfied?" Vanessa spoke her mind, just as always, and said, "You need to give his ass the Al Green treatment!" Yvette asked, "Vanessa, what the hell are you talking about?"

Vanessa quickly explained and said, "She needs to throw some hot grits on him. That's what I would do." Yvette said, "Vanessa, please shut up! So, Patricia, what are you going to do next? I mean, my main concern is that I think Andre crossed the line once he struck you." "Yeah, I know, but he apologized to me and promised it would never happen again. I guess I want to give him another chance." Vanessa said, "They all say they will never hit you again, or they simply apologize each time they hit you. Patricia, if he hits you once, he will most likely hit you again."

Patricia said, "I was concerned too at first, but I still believe Andre truly loves me. He just has a bad temper." "Yeah, that and he drinks like a Sailor!" Vanessa added. Vanessa was just being nosey as she asked Patricia, "Have you told your folks about this latest incident?" Patricia said, "No, because I did not want to upset them for nothing." She knew they would be upset with Andre. She knew her father would go after Andre if he knew what was going on. "Patricia, upset them for nothing? You call getting struck by your husband nothing?" Yvette said as she got up and paced the floor. Patricia replied, "Yvette, it was just a little fight.

I think Andre and I will be fine. Shit, you don't know what he has been through." Andre had snuck in without the girls hearing him. He had been standing at the doorway listening for a while. Not noticing Andre, Vanessa said, "If you ask me, I think he is crazy. From what you said about his childhood, he fits the profile of boys who grow up to be men who rape, kill, abuse, and goodness knows what else. His crazy ass probably does need some help." Vanessa noticed Patricia and Yvette looking over towards the door, their faces filled with a look of terror.

Vanessa turned around and saw Andre standing there with his arms on his hips. He appeared to be drunk already. "Patricia, I want those two bitches out of here!" Andre said with slurred speech. Vanessa jumped out of her seat and said, "Just who the hell are you calling a bitch?" Andre walked towards Vanessa and angrily said, "I am talking to you, bitch. Now leave! Yvette goes into her purse, pulls out some mace, and starts shaking the canister in preparation to use it. Vanessa jumped up, sending a punch to Andre's chest and a kick to his stomach.

Andre goes down as Vanessa falls back into a fighting stance. Andre, still sitting on the ground, takes a gun from his waistband and points it at Vanessa. Vanessa throws her hands up in the air in submission. Patricia said, "Vanessa and Yvette, I just need you two to leave. Please." "You want to attack me in my own house? Wrong answer! I can legally blow both your asses away!" Andre yelled. Vanessa slowly starts backing toward the door. Yvette soon follows. Vanessa opened the door, turned around, and said, "You need to teach your man some respect!" Andre had never feared a woman in his life, but he was afraid at that moment.

Yvette pulled Vanessa by the arm towards the door and asked, "Patricia, are you going to be all right?" Andre said, "She is going to be just fine as soon as you two get the hell out of my house!" As Vanessa left, she said, "If you need anything, girl, just give us a call. We will be over here in no time. I am about two seconds off his ass now!" Vanessa and Yvette do finally leave, as Andre looks at Patricia with disdain and says, "I thought I told you I don't want you with those two bitches." Patricia replied, "Andre, you said you do not like them, but you never told me I could not be friends with them or hang with them."

Andre did not like Patricia correcting him, so he gave her a dirty look and said, "Well, now I am telling you. I do not want you with them anymore!" Patricia said, "Baby, Yvette and Patricia are like my two sisters. We grew up together, and we have always been inseparable." She felt the need to convince Andre to change his mind. She knew she had to tread lightly because Andre was already pretty pissed. Andre said, "Yeah, right. They pretend to be your friends so they can know all your damn business. Shit, they know more about you and me than we do."

Patricia told Andre, "We do discuss various issues and problems together, but that is what girlfriends do." Andre wanted to isolate Patricia from her friends, believing this would be a good reason and a good opportunity. He said, "What happens in this house should stay in this house. It is nobody else's business." Patricia said, "Okay, baby, I will not discuss our problems with Yvette and Vanessa."

Andre still was not completely satisfied and said, "You need to include your nosy ass parents in that deal too." Patricia did not like Andre's request regarding her best friends, and she disliked the one regarding her parents even more. A lot more. Surely Andre could not be serious about what he was saying. She was very tight with her parents, especially her father. She could even discuss things with him that most girls would approach their mothers to talk about. "But you don't expect me to…" Patricia said. Andre once again cut her off and said, "I expect you to do whatever I tell you to do. I told you I am your husband, not your damn boyfriend. There is a big difference. Your ass belongs to me now." Andre walked up to Patricia, pushed her so hard she nearly fell backwards.

With his fists balled up, Andre asked, "You have anything else smart to say, you ungrateful bitch?" Patricia was nearly at a loss for words, but did say, "You promised not to treat me like this anymore." This angered Andre even more. He grabbed Patricia by her arm, pushed her back on the couch, and said, "Just sit your big ugly ass down and shut up!" Patricia got up to storm away once again. She was heading to the door with plans to visit her parents' house or one of her girlfriends' houses. She had some of her clothes and toiletries at each of the houses, so she was prepared to stay away from Andre if she had to.

Just as she made it to the door and opened it, Andre caught up to her. He grabbed her by her arm, spun her around with force, and said, "I am tired of you running to your damn parents' house all the time. You see, they spoil you and let you have your way, but I am not going that route with you! You are going to do what I tell you to, or I am going to make you pay." Patricia makes a futile attempt to get free of Andre's grasp, but she only makes him madder. He grabbed her and started shaking her violently like a rag doll.

Andre stopped shaking her momentarily, only to catch his breath. "Andre, I don't deserve this," Patricia said as she began to weep. Andre shoved Patricia into the wall so hard that he left her imprint on the wall. He said, "Oh, you deserve every bit of this bitch!" He threw Patricia on the couch and began to punch her all over her head and face. Patricia covered her head and face as best she could, hoping Andre would run out of gas or just stop beating her. He eventually ran out of gas. He walked away and went to bed as if nothing had even happened.

Later that night, Patricia did manage to make it over to Vanessa's house. Vanessa had a first aid kit with bandages and some ice packs. Patricia looked like she had gone several rounds with Mike Tyson. However, she did not go to the hospital. Yvette had also come over to Vanessa's house to give Patricia support. Patricia still attempts to explain it all away. She started by saying, "Andre just needs some help." Some of what she says is hard to understand. It is as if she is muttering words to herself. She appears to be in shock. Yvette said, "Patricia, don't be so naïve. I mean, Andre beat you up bad this time."

Vanessa applied an ice pack to Patricia's head and then wrapped a bandage loosely around her head to hold the ice in place. Vanessa said, "Now I am not a doctor. I am only familiar with the basics of first aid and CPR. Patricia, you sure you don't want to go to the hospital?" Patricia said, barely audibly, "No, I am fine." Yvette and Vanessa wanted to call the police so they could lock Andre up, at least for a while. Perhaps Patricia could then get a restraining order and some help. Yvette said, "Patricia, would you at least tell your parents?"

Even though she knew she and Vanessa had already told her parents. Patricia said, "No way, and you two better not either." Vanessa asked Patricia, "What are you going to do now?" Even Patricia realized at that point that something needed to be done. She didn't know what to do or where to go. Yvette and Vanessa could only go so far with Patricia, and they were limited in what they could do to help her. The decision to act was strictly in Patricia's hands. Vanessa said, "If you want, I can get some guys who will be more than happy to tighten his ass up for you. You just give me the word, girl."

Patricia quickly declined Vanessa's offer and said, "I do not want anyone else getting involved or getting into trouble." Vanessa just shook her head and said, "If you keep on letting him beat on you like this, you are the one who is going to need help." Patricia's cell phone rang, and it was Donna. Patricia shook her fist at Yvette and Vanessa. She knew they had told her parents. She said to Donna, "No, Mom, we just got in a little fight… No, I am okay… No, I do not want you and Daddy coming by… Okay, I will come by… Okay mom… I love you too… Goodbye."

After she finishes her conversation with Donna, she slams her flip phone shut and just gives Yvette and Vanessa a mean look. Patricia asked, "Now, why would you two tell my parents about what happened to me?" "We both thought it was best," answered Yvette. Patricia knew her two best friends were doing what was right, but for some reason, she still felt a sense of annoyance. To her, it was the principle of it that counted. She said, "I would expect Vanessa to do something like that, but not you, Yvette. Thanks a lot! Now I need to go home and explain all this shit to my parents. My father is going to go Rambo about this."

Patricia was distraught with her situation, but she was taking her frustrations out on her two best friends. Vanessa said, "Oh, girl, your parents would have found out about the abuse eventually one way or the other. You can't keep thinking your make-up will hide the problem from everyone. It goes a lot deeper than that." Right at that moment, Patricia reached into her bag, retrieved a mirror, and applied some makeup. She completely ignored what Vanessa said. She proceeded to put on the makeup rather heavily, especially around her bruises. She did not want her parents to see her in that condition.

Vanessa said, "Girl, why are you tripping about us trying to help you? We did it so you can get some help. You won't listen to us, so we thought maybe your parents would have a better shot at convincing you." Patricia got up to leave but stopped, turned around, and said, "Look, I am leaving. I will holler at you two another time. Bottom line is I thought I could trust you two, and you both let me down." Patricia left, and Yvette and Vanessa looked at each other, shaking their heads almost simultaneously. Vanessa said, "I guess we pissed her off."

Yvette said, "That is okay, she will get over it. I still say we did the right thing. She is probably going to thank us later." Later that evening, Patricia drove over to her parents' house. She stayed outside in her car for about two hours, trying to get up enough nerve to go inside. She just could not face them that night. She had cried much of her make-up away. She flipped down the sun visor and turned on the light in the vanity mirror. She stared at her face in the mirror for several minutes. She drove back to her house as she continued to cry like a baby.

Her cell phone rang repeatedly, but she did not bother to answer it. She knew it was her parents. She was obviously in no mood to explain her situation. She wanted to at least wait until the bruises and swelling in her face went down. She was hoping her father would not show up at her house. She would never put it past him. If he did, she was planning not to open the door. She did not believe that Andre would be bold enough to answer the door if Charles were to come over, either. She snuck into the house, knowing Andre was most likely sleeping. He was passed out on the couch, so fortunately, she was able to escape his wrath that night.

CHAPTER NINE

****

Andre came home from work and did his usual routine. He sat on the couch and grabbed the remote. Patricia had cleaned the house from top to bottom, and the dinner was cooked. Patricia was no longer working at her job. She had quit entirely and was allowing Andre to be the breadwinner as he requested. Patricia does get to see her friends from time to time. Sometimes she avoids confrontations with Andre by going to Vanessa's or Yvette's house.

There are sometimes periods of several days when Andre does not abuse or bother Patricia. There are times when he treats Patricia like a woman. Patricia still had to wonder whether she would be with Dr. Jekyll or Mr. Hyde. She did not know what to expect from Andre from one day to the next. As of that night, Andre had not beaten or verbally abused Patricia for quite a while. Patricia even had time to heal a bit. Therefore, she did finally get to see her parents. She was able to explain her problems with Andre away.

Unfortunately, this was going to be one of those bad nights. Andre had started drinking. He had begun drinking more heavily. The refrigerator was filled with beer, and the liquor cabinet had several bottles of liquor. Patricia could not say anything to him about it for several reasons. One, he would surely attack her; two, he was the one working, and finally, it was his money. "Bring me a beer!" Andre yelled at Patricia. Patricia brought Andre a beer. Andre opened the beer and gulped it down like a dehydrated man drinking water in the hot desert sun. "Bring me another one!" Andre shouted.

Patricia stood there for a few seconds. She pretty much knew what his heavy drinking would lead to. She hoped he would just pass out for the night like he often did when he drank. "Andre, you have not eaten dinner yet, are you sure you want another beer?" "Bring me a beer!" Andre demanded. Patricia is startled and quickly goes to the kitchen, coming back with a nice, cold beer for Andre. At that point, she began to sort of walk on eggshells. She was starting to learn what buttons set Andre off. Sometimes this helped, and other times it did not.

There were times when no matter what she said or did, she got either verbally or physically abused. Patricia had not had consensual sex with Andre since they were married. She struggled to find an emotional and physical connection with Andre that did not involve the abuse. That did not stop Andre from forcing himself on her on occasions. Andre managed to polish off a whole six-pack in less than half an hour and was feeling the effects.

"Come here," Andre said as he took his last gulp of his sixth beer. Patricia slowly and reluctantly approached Andre. She thought he was going to attack her. When she got close enough, Andre grabbed her by her arm and pulled her down on his lap. As she sat there in his lap, he began to grope her breasts and body. Patricia was not feeling particularly attractive and became somewhat resistant to Andre's advances. Andre began to get a little more aggressive, so Patricia felt she had better not resist. "What the hell is wrong with you? You're screwing another man, aren't you? That's why I don't want you with those two whores!" Andre growled. Patricia was quite shocked at such an accusation and said, "Baby, I would never cheat on you. I am just not feeling well now."

Andre threw Patricia on the couch and said, "You've been hanging around with those two bitches you call your friends, so there isn't any telling who you've been with! Patricia struggled with Andre at first, but then just lay there motionless. Andre starts tearing off Patricia's blouse. He then starts slapping her as he struggles to open her pants. Patricia covers her face as best she can as Andre tugs on her pants. He pulls her pants down nearly to her ankles. Patricia quickly slides her panties down and says, "Andre, you don't have to hurt me anymore. I will make love to you."

Andre slaps her once more and says, "Shut up! I am going to treat you like the whore you are!" Andre rapes Patricia violently. You can see the ferocity in his face. Patricia lies there motionless, allowing Andre to have his way. She knew that fighting Andre would be bad for her. Tears began to stream down her face, and blood flowed from her nose. Andre just got up, pulled his pants up, and walked away when he was finished. Patricia rolled over on her side and got into the fetal position. She began to cry out loudly as she rocked back and forth.

The next day, Yvette and Vanessa had managed to get Patricia to a Battered Women's Shelter. They take her to the office of Gina Perkins, the Program Coordinator. Gina is a rather tall African American female, thirty-five years old. Gina said, "Come on in, girls. I am Gina Perkins, the Program Coordinator here. I take it you are Patricia, right?" Patricia was not feeling this place. She replied to Gina sarcastically and said, "Lucky guess or did the bruises give me away?" Vanessa jumped right in and said, "Yeah, she is Patricia, this is Yvette, and my name is Vanessa. We are Patricia's two best friends. We are the ones who contacted your shelter."

Gina said, "You two are welcome to come by during visiting hours. Trust me, both of you did the right thing by bringing Patricia here." Patricia gave Yvette and Vanessa a group hug. "You two need to keep those cell phones on. I'm not sure if I'll stay here. I am just not feeling it," Patricia said as Vanessa and Yvette walked away. Yvette and Vanessa paid no attention to Patricia's statement as they continued walking away. They believed she was not talking rationally due to the abuse and was probably still in shock. Gina said, "Patricia, you have two great friends."

Patricia nodded in agreement. Gina felt she needed to ease Patricia's anxiety. Gina said, "Well, I guess we can start with a tour of our facility. Maybe we can meet some of the girls. Now our most important rule is that you have no contact with your husband or partner while you are here. That is for obvious safety reasons."

A young woman, named Michelle, walked down the hall of the facility. Michelle is a Caucasian female, about twenty-five years old. The bruises and black-and-blue marks on her face are noticeable. Michelle appears to have been battered violently. Gina stops Michelle before she passes by and says, "Michelle, how are you doing? Michelle, this is Patricia. Patricia, this is Michelle."

Michelle is somewhat embarrassed because of her appearance. She shakes Patricia's hand while looking down at the ground. She never really makes eye contact with Patricia or Gina. Michelle continued down the hallway very slowly and zombie-like. Patricia and Gina continue through the facility. Patricia asked, "Is that how the women here look?" "Some of them look like that, and some look even worse. Why?" "Well, I mean she was in pretty bad shape," replied Patricia.

Michelle was in considerably worse shape than Patricia, but only because Michelle had just arrived there today after her beating occurred. Gina said, "Oh, some of our girls are in bad shape. That is why we have a great nursing staff here as well as a great counseling staff. Sometimes, the internal or emotional wounds are far more severe than the physical wounds we can see. We need to help heal you from the inside out." Patricia took a deep breath, shook her head, and said, "Ms. Perkins, I don't think I belong here."

Gina was starting to get a little nervous at that point. Patricia had looked her right in the eyes and said those words. Gina felt she was going to lose Patricia from the shelter. Gina knew she needed to convince Patricia to stay. Gina asked, "Am I missing something? I mean, your husband does abuse you, right?" "Yeah, but it looks like her husband tried to kill her," Patricia replied. Gina could see that Patricia did not know how domestic violence usually goes. She wanted to make it very clear to Patricia.

Gina put her hand on Patricia's shoulder and said, "Just because your husband has not beaten you up that bad yet does not mean he won't. In most cases, the abuse gets progressively worse. Sometimes the woman even becomes a fatality." "Oh, please, Gina! I do not believe Andre would go that far. He just needs to get some help for his emotional problems. He has been through hell, but he has never received any help."

"Honey, they all need help in some way. Some are too far gone for help. Patricia, please don't be naïve. The cemeteries are full of women who thought their man would never kill them. Young lady, do you realize that every fifteen seconds in this country, an incident of domestic violence occurs?"

Patricia looked towards the floor and said, "Look, Ms. Perkins, I appreciate all your concern, but as I said, I don't feel I belong here. I think that maybe I would be taking a bed from someone who needs help." "Patricia, I cannot force you to stay. For you to get help, you must recognize the fact that you need help," Gina responded, with a tone of disappointment.

Patricia put out her hand and shook Gina's hand, and said, "Thanks, Gina, for your time, and I appreciate what you're trying to do for me and the other women." Gina holds Patricia's hand for a few seconds. She then reaches into her pocket with her free hand and gives Patricia a business card and a brochure of the facility. Gina said, "The National Domestic Violence hotline is on the brochure. You should get to know the number by heart." "Oh, I know it quite well, Ms. Perkins. It's 1-800-799-SAFE."

Patricia took out her cell phone and dialed Vanessa's number. "Girl, I need you to pick me up…This place is not where I need to be…Shit, I don't need a lecture right now! Please just come back and get me." Patricia yelled as she slammed her flip phone closed. Gina can see what is happening to Patricia. She feels Patricia is experiencing psychological stress and anxiety from the abuse. She said, "Patricia, are you sure you don't want to stay?" "No thanks, Ms. Perkins. I think I will be okay. My friends are going to come back and get me." Gina said, "Okay, you can wait for them in the lobby or my office if you want." "Ms. Perkins, I think I will just wait for them out front. Thanks again," Patricia said sadly.

Gina took out a pen and wrote her personal cell number on the back of the card and said, "Feel free to call me if you need to, but of course, if you have an emergency, don't hesitate to call nine-one-one. Now I can't promise you there will be space available for you later. Unfortunately, there is never a shortage of battered women in this community, just a shortage of shelters and facilities to house them. Many women use our facilities as a safe haven. You are welcome to use any of our resource centers or facilities at any time at no charge to you. Would you at least look at the facility with no obligations or strings attached?" Patricia looked around a little more and then said, "Gina, I will be fine. I will head outside now to wait for my friends." Patricia turned around and walked down the hall, her luggage in tow. Gina could only watch helplessly, and hope Patricia did not become a statistic or, much worse, a fatality.

CHAPTER TEN

****

Two days later, Andre was at home by himself. Patricia was staying with her parents once again. Andre planted several small hidden camera devices in various areas of the house. He then took out his phone to make sure the cameras were working. "Now I will be able to watch you and see everything you do in my house. And I better not see either one of those two bitches over here!" Andre said to himself.

Later that evening, Patricia made it back home. Andre went all out to welcome Patricia back home. He has cooked a full-course meal with candlelight provided, balloons, and a "Welcome home, Patricia" banner. The smooth sounds of Luther can be heard playing in the background. Patricia was sitting at the table, which was neatly made with a beautiful red tablecloth. Andre walked over and poured Patricia some Champagne. He bends down and gives Patricia a very warm kiss on the lips. Andre said, "Baby, I am so glad you came back home to me. I missed you. I thought I had lost you forever. You know I love you, right?"

Patricia nodded her head yes, but with notable uncertainty. Andre pulled up a chair, sat right next to Patricia, and said, "I just wanted to say I am sorry for the way I treated you and I wanted to make a solemn promise that I will never hurt you again." Andre left and came back with a bouquet of roses in a vase of water. Andre placed the roses right in front of Patricia. Patricia took the little card off the roses and read it aloud, saying, "I love you now and forever. You will always be special to me, with love, Andre Robinson."

Her words came out sort of distorted because her lips were still swollen from her previous encounter with Andre. The tears began to flow down Patricia's face. She said, "Andre, that is so sweet." "Hold on, baby, I have something else for you," Andre said as he ran back into the bedroom. He came back with a small box. He opened the box and presented Patricia with a beautiful gold necklace. "Honey, I hope you like this," he said as he put it around her neck. "Baby, I love it. It is so beautiful," Patricia said as she jumped up, hugged Andre, and continued, "Thank you so much, baby. I love you, too."

Andre then said, "I planned to wait until dinner was over to give you the gift, but I just could not wait. Now, baby, can you find it in your heart to forgive me?" Patricia asked, "Do you promise you won't hurt me anymore?" Andre said, "I will never hurt you again. That is my promise to you." Patricia then asked, "Would you go to marriage counseling with me or maybe see a counselor to help with your anger and nightmares?" Patricia did not feel it was an appropriate time to ask Andre that question.

Nevertheless, it was too late, and she just hoped it would not spoil the evening or set off Andre. Andre did not like Patricia asking him that question and replied, "I don't need any damn counseling! You think I am loco or something, right?" Patricia slowly slid backwards in her chair. She was afraid to reply to Andre or say anything else. She thought that maybe she would be better off and safer if she did not say anything. However, she did say, "No baby, I don't think you are loco. I just thought you might be able to get some help for your nightmares." At this point, she began to tremble with fear. She saw that look in Andre's eyes, and it was not a pretty sight for her.

Andre said, "I've been dealing with my nightmares for years. They don't even bother me anymore. We do not need a marriage counselor either. Our marriage is fine!" Patricia wanted to calm things down. She said, "Andre, let's not spoil the evening. I am sorry I brought it up. Let's just forget about it." Andre thought about it for a few seconds and pretty much agreed to let it go, but he was still clearly agitated.

Patricia wanted to make sure she got the subject off Andre's mind, so she changed the subject by asking Andre, "So honey, what did you cook tonight? It sure smells good." "I made some baked chicken, corn, rice, and some dinner rolls." "Yummy! Well, let's dig in before I starve to death," Patricia said. Andre brought the food in and set it on the table. As Andre sat down, Patricia reached over and held his hand. She bowed her head and said, "Thank you, Lord, for this food, which we are about to receive, for the nourishment of our bodies, for Christ's sake, amen." They both dug in. Patricia had a wonderful evening that night. She had almost managed to spoil a perfect evening. It was by far one of her best evenings with Andre to date.

Later that day, Patricia and Yvette arrived at Vanessa's house in a car. They exit the car and knock on Vanessa's door. Vanessa opens the door, allowing them to enter. Outside the home, Andre has parked his car and is watching the house with binoculars. He opens his glove box, pulls out a gun, and puts it on the front seat. He says to himself, angrily, "So, she is with those two bitches again! Well, I'm going to pay them a visit. I told her to stay away from them, but she just won't listen!"

Andre picks up the gun and opens the door to exit but then stops a while to think. He closes the car door and peels off, burning rubber. Patricia and Yvette sat on the couch. Patricia looked exhausted. "Are you two ready to do this routine or not?" Vanessa asked. Patricia looks at Yvette and says, "Well, I don't know about Yvette, but I am ready." "Oh, you all know me. I stay ready," Yvette responded. The ladies practice their dance routine, which looks well-rehearsed and sharp. The radio loudly plays upbeat dance music as they execute their dance moves with precision.

Patricia was at her parents' home about four weeks later. Things continue to get worse for Patricia the more she stays with Andre. She has once again sought shelter at her parents' house, waiting for Andre to sober up and calm down. Yvette and Vanessa are also there. Patricia has fresh bruises on top of the older, healing ones. She even has stitches over her right eye. Donna left the living room and came back with a hand mirror. Donna held the mirror right in front of Patricia and said, "Patricia, just look at your face. Honey, this is not love."

Patricia quickly turned away as if she had seen a ghost. "No, I want you to take a good, long, hard look at your face! Don't turn away, I want you to see this," Donna said. Charles got out of his seat and was pacing back and forth like a ferocious caged lion. He is livid as he says, "Patricia, this is a vicious cycle. He beats you; you come stay with us or your friends for a short period, and then you go right back to him. What could you possibly see in him at this point? You know he is not going to change." Patricia emphatically said, "I still love him, and I am not ready to throw the towel in on my marriage just yet. You don't know Andre like I do."

"Patricia, this guy is no good for you, and I think you know it. He has already been through two wives, most likely because he is an abuser. Now he is trying to make you the third abused ex-wife," Charles said. Vanessa was sitting on the couch right next to Patricia. She wanted to make sure Patricia heard what she had to say. She got Patricia's attention by looking her right in the face and saying, "How long are you going to let this go on? Shoot, the police and Paramedics come to your house so often they are talking about making it one of their substations."

Yvette and Patricia's parents did not like that statement and didn't find any humor in it. Even though Vanessa was acting very serious, it seemed she was trying to slide in a little of her comical twist, as she often did. Needless to say, her timing was wrong. Yvette said, "You still don't think you need to get some help or go to a shelter? I am sure you are starting to look just like some of those women you saw. Remember the ones you said needed help?" Vanessa jumped up and said, "I think he needs an attitude adjustment. I told you I know a few friends who would take care of his ass! No questions asked. I could do it myself, but he ain't worth a trip to jail."

Suddenly, Charles jumped up, grabbed his Louisville Slugger bat, and headed to the door. Vanessa follows right behind him as if she wants a piece of the action, too. Charles said, "Shit, I can take care of his ass myself!" Donna caught up to Charles and snatched the bat away from him. She asked Charles, "Baby, have you lost your mind?" Charles said, "I just wanted to talk to Andre." Charles headed back to his seat and continued, saying, "What the hell am I supposed to do? That son-of-a-bitch is hurting Patricia!"

Vanessa quickly returned to her seat, sat down, and acted as if she were not part of the outburst. "Honey, I guess you have lost your mind. You are not acting any better than him now," Donna said as she sat down next to Charles with the Louisville Slugger still in her hand. "Look, I just want to go face-to-face and toe-to-toe with him and find out what his problem is," Charles said. Donna said, "If you go out there with this bat, you would be doing the wrong thing, and I think you know it." "Well, I am tired of sitting around and doing nothing," Charles said.

Donna said, "Believe me, Charles, you are not the only one who feels like that. We'd all love to go down there and have a piece of Andre. I can't let you do this. What good would it do? You would be in jail for assaulting him, and he would still be beating Patricia." Patricia had listened long enough and finally said, "Look, I don't want any of you to get involved. He knows you all are trying to get me away from him, and believe me, he is pissed about it." Charles replied, "Oh, he is pissed, huh? He does not know what pissed is until I get hold of him! I will show his ass pissed."

Donna asked, "Patricia, do you believe Andre would be bold enough to come after us? Is that what you are trying to say?" Patricia said, "I am not sure because sometimes Andre gets pretty crazy." Charles said, "You need to get away from that crazy fool!" "There is something else I need to tell you all," Patricia said as tears began to stream down her face again. Everyone silently waited in anticipation to hear what Patricia had to say. As Patricia paused for a while so she could get the words out, there was a moment of silence. She finally was able to say, "I am pregnant." Charles said, "Patricia, you are joking, right?" "No, Dad, I am very serious," Patricia responded.

Charles said, "Well, you two certainly did not waste any time!" They were not as happy about the news as friends and family usually would be on such an occasion. They all knew Andre was no good for Patricia, and now she was going to have a child by him. It was even clear by the way Patricia delivered the news that she was not even happy about it. Donna said, "Patricia, what were you thinking about? Certainly, you could not have been thinking straight or rationally." "Well, I did not want it to happen so soon, but it did. So that is where we are now. How do we know that this baby won't change Andre? Now, I am going to have Andre's baby, so can we move on?"

Patricia could never tell them how this baby was conceived. She felt she could never let them know about the vicious rape. Andre got pleasure out of forcing her to have sex with him while he battered and abused her. Even if Patricia did not resist, Andre was still aggressive. Sometimes it seemed like he was even more aggressive when she didn't fight back. Patricia was just never in the mood for Andre. He no longer turned her on. He felt he had the right to take that part of her because he believed she was his property.

Charles said, "Andre is going to be a part of you and that baby's life in some way for a long time." Patricia was overwhelmed with emotion and hurt as she said, "Look, I am confused now, so can I just have a moment alone? Please!" Charles stood up and said, "Okay, everybody, let's give her some space." Charles escorted Yvette and Vanessa to the door. Patricia lies on the couch and begins to cry out loudly. Charles and Donna try to console her at first, but then they walk away, allowing her to get everything out.

CHAPTER ELEVEN

****

The next day, Patricia went back home, but she was reluctant to go inside. She waited outside for over an hour, trying to get the courage to face Andre. She noticed the beer boxes and bottles outside in the trash. It seemed Andre had a party, but that wasn't the case. He had been drinking heavily. Patricia had hoped perhaps he was fast asleep from his alcohol consumption. It was getting late, and Patricia was getting tired of waiting outside.

She knew she had few choices. She could sleep outside, go to crazy Vanessa's house, or go to her somewhat worrisome parents' house. Yvette's house or a battered woman's shelter was out of the question. She didn't want to stay in a hotel because Andre was the breadwinner now, and she didn't want to borrow money from her parents or friends. She chose to risk a beating and go inside. She quietly opened the front door and began tiptoeing through the house. She carried a small flashlight with her, which she used to sneak through the house.

Andre slept hard when he drank. However, turning on the lights would usually wake him. Andre was passed out on the couch in his usual spot, with his work clothes still on. Emptied beer bottles littered the coffee table. He appeared to be waking up, so Patricia stopped dead in her tracks and froze.

She waited for Andre to stop moving around, and then she continued to the bedroom. She felt that she had once again avoided a confrontation with Andre. Sometimes she preferred him drunk like that. He was usually too drunk to rape her or beat her up. She was beginning to feel physically and psychologically burned out.

Essentially, she was so stressed that she was struggling to stay focused. She was terrified of Andre, but even more afraid to make a move. She was scared to come home to Andre or to go home at all. It didn't feel like home. It felt more like hell, and Andre was the Devil. Patricia was in bed sleeping when she heard things being thrown around and broken. Andre had woken up and gone on a rampage. Patricia just lay there for a while, hoping he would stop and go back to sleep. It was about one-thirty in the morning, and Andre was supposed to be up for work in less than four hours.

Patricia was afraid to confront Andre. She got her cell phone ready in case she had to call the police. She was hoping it wouldn't get to that point, but she certainly wanted to be prepared. Andre managed to work his way to the back room, where Patricia was. Patricia had already started getting ready to leave. Her bag was already packed, as she was prepared for these confrontations. Patricia hoped she could just get out of there with no problems. Andre grabbed Patricia and punched her like she was a man.

Patricia went down, and Andre started kicking and beating her. Andre yelled, "I am going to teach you a lesson because you are a no-good bitch, and you don't listen to me!" Patricia went motionless as she lay there on the floor. Andre attempts to awaken Patricia, but she remains still. Suddenly, there is a loud knock at the door. Two black female officers are standing outside with their hands on their weapons. Officer Powell is about five feet nine, thirty-two, and tough-looking. Officer McNeil is the less rugged looking of the two. She is approximately 28 years old and stands at about 5 feet 6 inches. She was smaller than Officer Powell, but she was just as tough.

Andre yelled, "Who is it?" Officer McNeil yelled, "It's the police! Now open the door before we have to open it for you!" Andre slowly opened the door and said, "What is the problem, officer? We did not call the police." Officer McNeil wanted to make sure Andre knew precisely who they were because they were in plain clothes. She said, "First of all, I am Officer McNeil, and this is my partner, Officer Powell. We are from the DVTF unit, or the Domestic Violence Task Force. We are here because your neighbors called about a four-fifteen here." Andre asked, "What the hell is a four-fifteen?"

He knew precisely what a four-fifteen was, but he was just playing dumb. A female officer duo had never arrested him, so he felt he could take advantage of them. After all, he was used to being in control when it came to women. Officer Powell asked, "Are you fighting with your wife again, Mr. Robinson?" Officer McNeil heard a faint woman's cry coming from the back room as she walked down the long hallway. She rushes into the bedroom and sees Patricia on the floor. Officer McNeil yelled out to Officer Powell, "Hook him up! We have a female down back here!"

Officer McNeil assessed Patricia's condition and said, "Ma'am, I need you to stay still. Help is coming." She got on her two-way radio and said, "Dispatch, this is Officer McNeil, roll rescue to this location for a female down. Advise response to be code three. Roll a black-and-white to this location also for the transport of one male suspect. Stand by for our status. Officer Powell, do you need assistance with the arrest?" Officer Powell said, "No, I am good. I can handle it."

Officer McNeil knew Officer Powell could handle herself very well. She just thought she would ask anyway. Back in the living room, Andre has taken a somewhat fighting stance towards Officer Powell. Officer Powell yelled at Andre, "Turn around and put your hands on your head! Do it now because that is the only warning you will get!" Andre started slowly walking towards Officer Powell with his fists up and said, "You don't have the right to be in my house, so get the hell out of here bitch before I have to show you who is in charge here. This is my house, damn it, and I run things here!"

Andre throws a punch at Officer Powell, which is a huge mistake. Officer Powell is not Patricia. Officer Powell grabbed Andre's arm and did a Judo expert-type take-down. Andre hits the floor hard. She rolled Andre over, put her knee in his back, and handcuffed him. Officer McNeil has heard the commotion and, as a result, knows what happened. She asked, "Is the suspect okay or do we need to double-up on rescue transport?" Officer Powell responds, "Negative on the second rescue unit. Advise dispatch our status is code four at this location with one in custody."

She stands Andre up and says, "Perhaps you needed a lesson on how to treat women. More importantly, you better know which one you are stepping to. I am not your wife!" Andre still struggles and said, "My wife fell, and I was just getting ready to call the ambulance when you all came." Officer Powell just shook her head and said, "Yeah, right, and she landed on her face about a dozen times. Tell it to the judge! Right now, you have the right to remain silent; use it. Anything you say or do can be used against you in the court of law. You have the right to an attorney and to have him present during questioning.

Officer Powell continued reading Andre his rights, saying, "If you cannot afford an attorney, one will be appointed for you. Do you understand your rights?" Andre said, "Yeah, I understand. I think you dislocated my shoulder bitch!" Officer Powell said, "I am not going to be too many more bitches. Now I suggest you zip it before I have to take you down again. Trust me, the first time was nothing." Andre wisely kept his mouth shut. The Paramedics finally arrived and assisted Patricia. They are two African American men, whose names are Brad and Roy. Both were in their late twenties.

As Patricia was wheeled out of the house, two uniformed officers came in. One was a large black man in his late thirties. His partner was a smaller, white man in his early forties. Andre was handed over to them, and they escorted him out. Officer McNeil comforted Patricia as she was put inside the ambulance. A few nosey neighbors appear outside, even at that late hour. Red and blue lights illuminate the neighborhood. Andre is placed in a marked patrol car and driven away. Simultaneously, the ambulance drives up the block in the opposite direction to the hospital.

Patricia arrived at Tri-County Hospital. The two Paramedics rushed Patricia down a hospital hallway and into an emergency room. Doctor Richardson and several nurses were present in the emergency room. Doctor Richardson, a middle-aged Caucasian male, checks Patricia out and asks, "How long has she been out?" Brad replied, "She has been coming in and out of consciousness. Her vitals appear to be normal." Doctor Richardson continued to assess Patricia's condition and asked, "What happened to her? Is this the motor vehicle accident victim?" Roy said, "No, this is the domestic violence victim."

Yvette and Vanessa came rushing through the hospital. Patricia managed to call them while Andre was tossing stuff around the house. Patricia still refused to call her parents or involve them. Yvette had planned for Patricia to meet her and Vanessa outside her home. They were going to pretty much rescue her from Andre, at least for the night. They did make it to Patricia's house only to see her being rolled into the ambulance. They followed the ambulance to the hospital while going through every red light.

Yvette called Patricia's parents while they were chasing the ambulance to the hospital. Therefore, it would not be too long before they arrived at the hospital. Patricia's parents lived quite close to the hospital. Officer McNeil and Officer Powell arrived shortly thereafter, followed by Donna and Charles. Patricia's friends are already waiting in the waiting area. They wanted to check on Patricia, but they were not her immediate family. Donna and Charles rushed into the Hospital emergency room area. Donna was still in her nightclothes, slippers, and robe. "Where is Patricia Robinson?" Charles asked the receptionist.

The Receptionist, a young Caucasian female in her twenties, asked, "Are you folks Patricia's parents?" "Yes, we are Patricia's parents," Charles replied. The receptionist said, "Have a seat in the waiting room, and I will have a doctor or nurse update you on Patricia's status." Donna and Charles went into the waiting area, where they met up with Yvette and Vanessa. After they all embraced each other for support, they began pacing the floor alongside Charles. Doctor Richardson came into the waiting area to brief Patricia's parents.

They all surround the doctor like a football team in a huddle, and Charles asks, "Is she going to be okay?" Doctor Richardson said, "We have her stabilized at this time. She got beat up badly, so she does have bruises, contusions, and a few lacerations. We are going to have to keep her overnight for further tests and evaluations." They all tried to speak at once, and the doctor said, "I cannot help much if you all speak at the same time." After there was a short moment of silence, Donna asked, "May we go back and see her?"

Doctor Richardson said, "Not until tomorrow. She needs to get some rest now, so we have her sedated. We will keep a watchful eye on her. Believe me, she is in good hands, and I believe she will make a full recovery. We will let you know if we find anything that might change that statement because everything is still in the preliminary stages." They all collectively sigh in relief. They all decided to stay at the hospital and wait for any changes in Patricia's condition. None of them believed they would be able to sleep anyway until they were sure Patricia had pulled through.

Donna said, "Doctor Patricia is pregnant. Will your tests be able to determine if the baby is okay?" "Well, we will do an ultrasound and some other tests on her, but as I said, it is still early now. Now, is she on any meds or allergic to any meds?" Donna said, "No, she is not taking anything, and I don't believe she is allergic to anything." "Okay, folks, I need to get back to my patients. We will keep you advised," Doctor Richardson said as he walked towards the double doors leading to the emergency room treatment area.

As Doctor Richardson left, they all took seats to wait it out. Morning came quickly as they all fell asleep. One of the black nurses came out and said, "I need to speak to the parents of Patricia Robinson." Donna and Charles jumped up to greet the nurse for an update on Patricia's condition. Yvette and Vanessa, not being Patricia's parents, also jump up in unison. "We are her sisters!" Vanessa yelled. The nurse said, "She is still in pain, but she is doing a lot better. You can go back and see her briefly because she is talking." They all are led back to Patricia's room. Patricia is sitting up in her bed. She looks bad, but she seems to be conscious and alert.

The nurse checks to make sure Patricia is still okay. Donna gives Patricia a long hug and asks, "You okay, baby?" Patricia said, "I guess so. I feel like I've been toe-to-toe with Muhammad Ali. Nurse, I need something for my pain." The nurse replied, "I have your sedative right here. Do you want it now or after your family leaves? They will not be able to stay too long." Patricia said, "I think I can hang on for a while." The Nurse adjusted Patricia's pillows and said, "I will be back in about ten minutes. Patricia, if you need us, you can push the button. If you all want more time with her, you have to come during visiting hours."

After the nurse left, Charles put things in perspective by saying, "Your fight was not with Mohammed Ali, it was with Andre Robinson." "What are you going to do now, Patricia?" Donna asked. "I don't know. I am still afraid and confused," Patricia replied. Charles said, "Baby, we do not have to discuss the incident with you now. If you want to get some medicine for your pain and get some sleep, we can come back later." Patricia adjusted some pillows behind her and asked, "Where is Andre?" Charles said, "He was arrested, but he will probably be out and back home before you get out of here."

Doctor Richardson came in to adjust Patricia's IV. Patricia said, "I guess Andre and I need to try to work this out." Dr. Richardson had to do a double-take. He couldn't believe he had heard Patricia correctly. He had seen many abused women come through the emergency room, and some of them did not make it. Doctor Richardson could no longer remain silent and said, "Young lady, I hate to get in your family business, but I just can't stand here and listen to you without wanting to give you some sound advice. Now, I wish I could show you some pictures of abused women who come through these doors nearly every day."

Doctor Richardson continued, saying, "Some don't even make it. Do yourself and your loved ones a favor. Get out of this situation or get some help before it is too late. Things are unlikely to improve, but they are more likely to deteriorate. Now I will step out and let you folks have some time alone with Patricia. Once again, I am sorry for butting in." Charles said, "No, we appreciate your input. It was good for Patricia to hear that from your viewpoint as a doctor."

As Doctor Richardson was leaving, he stopped, turned around, and said, "I can help with healing your physical injuries, but I can't help you with the emotional and psychological trauma you undoubtedly have. That usually runs a lot deeper than your physical trauma." As Doctor Richardson was leaving, Officer McNeil and Officer Powell walked in. They are there to get an official statement from Patricia.

Officer Powell asked, "Doctor, is it okay to interview Patricia quickly?" Doctor Richardson said, "Yeah, that should be okay while things are fresh in her head. She is in pain now, so please try to be brief." Doctor Richardson left. Officer McNeil said, "I am Officer McNeil, and this is my partner, Officer Powell. We are detectives from the DVTF, or Domestic Violence Task Force. We are just here to get a formal statement from Patricia. It should not take too long." Charles asked, "Is it okay for us to stay, or do you need privacy to speak with Patricia?" Officer McNeil said, "It is okay if you stay because Patricia needs a lot of support now." Officer Powell took out a pen and small notepad and said, "Actually, we wanted to ask Patricia a few questions about what happened to her so we can do our report."

Patricia said, "Well, basically it was no big deal. We just had an argument and a fight. He just has some problems, and sometimes he drinks too much." Officer McNeil looked at Officer Powell and everyone else in the room, shook her head, and said, "What do you mean it was no big deal? You would not be here if it were no big deal." Patricia said, "I am not going to press charges on him if that is what you all want. It will only make him angrier, and then I am the one who will have to deal with him." Charles told Patricia, "What are you talking about, Patricia? This guy beat you unconscious."

Donna began to cry and said, "Patricia, please do not let this continue. Please, baby, we can't stand seeing you like this. Andre is not going to stop hurting you. He has to be stopped." Charles hugged Donna and tried to console her. Yvette also tried to comfort Donna by hugging her and saying, "Everything will be okay." Patricia asked, "Is he down at County again?" "Yes, he is probably being booked in now. From his record, you are not his first victim. It seems Mr. Robinson has a history of domestic violence charges involving his other now ex-wives," Officer McNeil said. Donna said, "No wonder he does not like to talk about them." He was beating them, too."

Patricia asked, "Yeah, but they are still alive, right?" Officer Powell said, "They both are alive, but what does that have to do with anything?" Patricia said, "Well, everyone seems to think Andre is going to kill me or something. Andre may need some help, but he is not a killer. Maybe we should just give him the benefit of the doubt." "Girl, what did that doctor give you? It must be something that got you still tripping," Vanessa said. Yvette and Donna looked at Vanessa as if she had said something bad. Charles was not surprised, as he generally agreed with Vanessa's views.

The two of them were very close in their thinking about Patricia's abuse. Neither one of them bit their tongues on the issues, nor did they hesitate to say how they felt at any given time. Officer McNeil and Officer Powell looked at each other and shrugged their shoulders. They certainly were no strangers to domestic violence situations. They were seasoned officers on the police force and the DVTF unit. Charles added, "By the way, I believe we have given Andre more than the benefit of the doubt." "So, what happens to him now? Is he going to do time for this?" Patricia asked.

Officer McNeil said, "He will have to attend the brand new, mandatory stress and anger management course, which all abuse suspects have to go through. The evidence is quite clear that he abused you. I mean, he has been arrested for battering you several times already. Each time you refuse to press charges, he wins and manages to take a little more from you."

Officer Powell added, "Statistically, the course has a very low success rate. Most of the abusers go right back to abusing. However, the program is state-mandated. The old theory of locking them all up and throwing away the key no longer applies. The state feels there must be some sort of intervention or rehab for domestic violence suspects. The sad thing is that those courses are always full. It could take months for him to get in."

Patricia rolled over like she was going to sleep. She asked, "So what do you want from me?" Officer McNeil told Patricia, "As we said before, we need a statement. Please don't tell us you ran into a wall or fell. Do not waste our time by trying to insult our intelligence." "You know what happened! Maybe I don't feel like discussing it now," Patricia declared.

Donna said, "Honey, we do need to discuss this. We love you and we are concerned about you." Patricia said, "You just do not understand. I don't think any of you understand." Patricia pressed her service button and said, "Look, I just want the doctor or nurse to come back and give me something for this pain." Officer Powell said, "Okay, Patricia, we will leave and let you get some rest." Officer McNeil reached into her pocket and pulled out a card. She pulled out a pen and wrote the number to the National Domestic Violence Hotline.

She wrote 1-800-799-SAFE and said, "That line is available twenty-four hours. Do not hesitate to call nine-one-one if you need immediate assistance." It was almost like Patricia was ignoring the officers as she took the card, tossed it on the nightstand, and asked, "So when do I get to see my husband?" Officer Powell responded by saying, "Hopefully not before the ink dries on our reports. He is being booked on resisting arrest and attempted assault on a police officer. That should keep him behind bars quite a bit longer." Patricia said, "Thank you, officers." She pressed the service button once again. The officers left looking sort of dejected and defeated. They felt they could not reach Patricia.

Patricia rolled back over, this time facing away from everyone. She assumed her favorite stress-relieving position, the fetal position. She began to cry loudly. "It's going to be alright, Patricia. We are all here for you, and we will support you through this difficult time. You just get better, baby," Donna said as she rubbed Patricia's back. Yvette started to cry, and for the first time, Vanessa was overcome with emotion and began to cry as well. They all hugged Patricia and then left.

CHAPTER TWELVE

****

Three days later, Patricia was back at Vanessa's house. Yvette was there also. Patricia stands up and puts her hand on her hip. "So, are we going to do this new dance routine or what?" Patricia asked. Vanessa and Yvette looked at Patricia, then at each other. "No, we are not doing any dance routine today," Vanessa said, with a somber tone. "Then, what are we doing?" Patricia asked, with a puzzled look. She could tell by the look on their faces that they were up to no good.

"Well, you know my brother was a fourth-degree black belt and taught me for many years, right?" Vanessa asked. "Yes, we know that! And your point?" Patricia responded with an attitude. "This is something I should have done a long time ago. I am going to teach you some self-defense techniques." Vanessa said with confidence. "So, you think I am going to just be able to beat the crap out of my husband? Then what? You think he will stop pursuing me, and I will live happily ever after?" Patricia asked, with some sarcasm in her tone.

Vanessa looked over at Yvette. She knew Yvette would be able to convince Patricia. Yvette said, "Look, it's better to be prepared to defend yourself. I mean, you don't plan on leaving him, right? Please let her help you. I mean, it won't hurt you to be ready for him. At this point, it's not a matter of if but when you may need it." "Okay! Okay! I'll do it!" Patricia finally agreed. Vanessa looked at Yvette and gave her a half-smile and a nod. "Well, I will sit back and watch you two. I don't need to learn karate. My husband and I are just fine. I'm pretty sure, at this point, that he won't be attacking me." Yvette said as she flopped back in the recliner.

"No, Yvette, you know we do everything together. This is no different. This is not just about whether your husband attacks you or not. What about being attacked by someone, period? On your feet, girl!" said Vanessa. Yvette popped up rather quickly and appeared ready to get started. "Okay, let's do this!" Yvette shouted. Vanessa fell back into a fighting stance. Yvette and Patricia did the same. "Well, this is for hand-to-hand combat. You're at a huge disadvantage if he gets to his gun."

Vanessa continued, "But I can show you some techniques to disarm him if you're close to him when he pulls his gun. But these are risky techniques." Vanessa said confidently, proceeding to execute some quick kicks and punches. "What do you mean by risky techniques? Do you mean if they don't work, I'm dead?" Patricia asked with a puzzled look. "Oh, Patricia, stop being such a drama Queen! Vanessa is just trying to help you!" Yvette said while shaking her head. "Okay, well, let's go! I'm ready," Patricia yelled out. "But don't y'all go crazy. I'm pregnant, remember?" Patricia continued.

Vanessa once again dropped back into a fighting stance, as Patricia and Yvette did the same. Vanessa led them with some kicking and punching techniques. "The first thing you want to do to protect yourself from an attack or assault is to get into a fighting stance. From here, you can be ready to block for defense or punch and kick to counterattack or neutralize. You may not always have the time to get into a stance, so you should always be ready," Vanessa explained. Patricia, with a puzzled look, asks, "Shouldn't we do some stretches or maybe warm up first?"

Vanessa briefly gets out of her fighting stance but quickly snaps back into it. Vanessa responds to Patricia by saying, "Remember what I said. You need to always be ready. You most likely will not have the time to stretch if that fool suddenly attacks you." Vanessa leads the ladies in practicing some self-defense techniques.

A few days later, Andre was sitting in his car, parked outside of Patricia's parents' home. Charles had seen him sitting there after peeking out the kitchen window. Andre opens his glove box, pulls out a gun, and says to himself, "Time for me to set your ass straight about Patricia and me!"

Charles walks outside and to the end of the driveway. He is carrying his Louisville Slugger bat as he stands there watching Andre. Andre puts the gun in his waistband, exits his car, and walks toward Charles. Charles points the bat at Andre and says, "What the hell are you doing here? You've got some nerve coming over here to my house. Now I suggest you get your ass out of here. The police are on their way!" "I was thinking that maybe it's time we have a man-to-man talk about Patricia," Andre said, as he slowly reached for the gun that was in his waistband.

Andre grabbed the handle of the weapon, but he did not pull it out of his waistband. Charles takes one or two steps forward. He once again points the bat at Andre and says, "There is nothing for us to discuss, other than if you put your hands on her again, I will beat the brakes off you. Now, get away from my house. You are no longer welcome here!"

Suddenly, an unmarked police car screeches onto the scene, with flashing lights. Officer Powell and Officer McNeil step out and approach Andre with their weapons drawn. Andre puts his hands up, not wanting to risk being shot. "He came over here saying we need to discuss my daughter!" Charles roared.

While still pointing her weapon at Andre, Officer Powell says, "Sir, can you do us a favor and drop the bat?" Charles quickly tosses the bat aside. With his hands still in the air, Andre says, "I was trying to get to know my father-in-law a little better." "Turn around!" Officer McNeil said with an authoritative voice. Andre does not do what he is told. "Am I under arrest?" Andre asked. Officer Powell says, "I suggest you do what you're told. You know what happened last time you resisted." Andre turns around.

Officer McNeil holsters her gun, pushes Andre up against the police car, and handcuffs him. She then asks, "Do you have anything that will poke me?" Andre busts out laughing and says, "Yeah, it's about eight inches and it's in my pants. I'm pretty sure if it pokes you, you would like it." He then laughs again. Officer McNeil pushes Andre up against the car and begins to search him, as she warns him, saying, "You really should use your right to remain silent. I'm not in the mood for your shit today!"

Officer McNeil lifts Andre's shirt and sees the gun in his waistband. "He has a gun!" She shouts. With a serious expression, Andre shakes his head and says, "I brought my gun with me because this is not the safest neighborhood." Officer McNeil puts the gun on the roof of the car as she finishes up her search. Charles becomes visibly upset and says, "You mean he came over here to confront me and he has a gun?" "Yes, and this could have ended differently if we had not gotten here when we did," said Officer Powell, finally holstering her gun. Officer McNeil reads Andre his rights and puts him into the police car. She gets in the driver's seat, and Officer Powell gets in the front passenger seat as they then drive off.

Charles retrieves his Louisville Slugger bat, shakes his head, and goes back into his house. Two weeks later, it was girls' night out for Patricia, Vanessa, and Yvette. They were finally getting the chance to hang out together. They were at a nightclub called Club Elegance. Slow music can be heard playing in the background as DJ Rob Smooth says, "I will be the host for the night, representing 104.9FM, the oldies beat station." DJ Rob Smooth resembled a shorter version of Heavy D. Patricia looked somewhat tense.

This was a mandatory fun night, and Vanessa and Yvette were not going to let Patricia stay in a gloomy mood. Vanessa said, "Girl, you need to loosen up a bit. We brought you out here to have some fun, and damn it, you are going to have some fun!" Patricia pulled out a small, portable lighted vanity mirror, looked at her face, and said, "Do I look okay? My face looks okay, right?" Vanessa said, "Your face looks fine. You sure put enough makeup on. Shit, you look like the damn Joker." Patricia was looking around the club, as if she were expecting someone. She just was not sure if Andre would show up. She is nervous about being out with her friends. Andre was definitely on her mind.

Vanessa said, "Girl, I told you to stop tripping when you are out with us. That fool is not going to show up in here with all these potential witnesses! He would be crazy to try something like that. Besides, if he does, you know we've got your back. You know we can't stand his trifling ass anyway." Patricia surprises Yvette and Vanessa when she defends Andre by saying, "Vanessa, I wish you wouldn't disrespect my husband like that." Vanessa and Yvette just sat there for a few seconds, looking at Patricia with their mouths open. They just do not know what it will take to get through to her.

Vanessa wanted to respond to what Patricia had said. However, she was not going to let an argument about Andre spoil their evening. Not on this special occasion. Yvette said, "We came here to have a good time. So, let's leave our baggage and relationship woes behind us and have some damn fun!" Vanessa agreed with Yvette and said, "Yeah, that is true. We came here to party, so let's do this! Shit, you know I am ready to get my groove on. Just look at all these fine brothers in here." Yvette said, "I will be right back. I need to speak to DJ Rob Smooth. Remember, Patricia, this is our night."

Yvette returned to the table and sat down with a big smile on her face. She knew just what would get all of them on the dance floor. It was sort of like an anthem for the girls. As the music fades out, DJ Rob Smooth says, "Don't forget to come on out and enjoy Hip-hop and reggae night here at Club Elegance every Saturday with drink specials until eleven. This next song goes out to Patricia Robinson from her best friends, Yvette and Vanessa. It's called "Lady's Night" by Kool and the Gang. This is Flash-back Friday, and I am DJ Rob Smooth from FM-one-zero-four point nine."

DJ Rob Smooth spins the record. Yvette and Vanessa pulled Patricia onto the dance floor. The crowd opens up the dance floor like the Red Sea. It was as if they knew that these three sisters needed the space. The girls do a very nice dance routine. They dance so well together, and it is clear the routine was well rehearsed. You can see how strong their friendship is, as Patricia smiles and has a good time. For that moment, Yvette and Vanessa had made Patricia have fun and forget about her problems with Andre.

A few days later, sadly, Patricia went back home to Andre once again. Andre sat Patricia on the couch and said, "Okay, baby, now cover your eyes. No peeking." He rushes to the closet and retrieves several boxes. At that point, Patricia's pregnancy was quite noticeable, and she was showing. "Okay, you can open your eyes now," Andre said as he set the boxes on the couch. "Wow, honey, what is all this?" Patricia asked as her eyes widened. Andre said, "I have a few gifts for you, baby. Go ahead and open them up." Patricia hugged Andre.

She tore open the box like a child on Christmas morning. The first box contained two beautiful dresses. "Thank you, baby, I love them," Patricia said, putting the dresses up against her body to see how they would look on her. Andre said, "Then I am sure you will love the rest." Patricia proceeded to open the following few boxes at the same time, as they contained shoes. She received three sets of very fashionable shoes. As Patricia began to slip on the shoes and try on each pair, she said, "What is today? Did I forget some special occasion or something? I know it is not my birthday, and I know it is not our anniversary." Andre said, "No, baby, I just wanted to show you how much I love you."

Patricia hugged Andre again and said, "Oh, Andre, you are so sweet." Patricia opened the rest of the boxes, which were considerably smaller in size. Those boxes contained a beautiful watch and several articles of jewelry of unspecified value. He also gave her a wad of cash. He would often give her a sort of allowance. He did not know Patricia was saving the money. Patricia said, "Baby, I am somewhat speechless." She gave Andre one last long hug and said, "I love everything, baby. Thank you, but I feel bad because I did not get anything for you."

Andre spun Patricia around and said, "I am sure you have something I might like to have a little later tonight." He smiled, winked, pulled Patricia close to him, and said, "Maybe a little later with me, you and some Luther." Patricia said, "Andre, I am just not feeling sexual tonight." Patricia put her hand over her mouth as if she did not want that to come out. She felt that once again she would be spoiling a perfect evening and possibly ruffling Andre's feathers. Andre pretty much ignored Patricia's comment. He knew she would not have consensual sex with him. However, he was trying to appear romantic so she would forgive him again.

Andre said, "Well, you don't have to cook tonight, baby." Patricia was surprised and asked, "Why, baby? Aren't you hungry?" "Yes, I am starving but tonight is a Red Lobster night. Dinner is on me." Patricia hugged Andre, gave him a nice, long kiss, and said, "Thanks for everything, Andre. You made my day." Later that night, Andre took Patricia back to the restaurant where they had their first date. He also took her dancing; despite knowing she would likely outshine him on the dance floor.

CHAPTER THIRTEEN

****

Patricia was at home with Andre about two months later. Andre had been relatively passive to date. She was showing significantly now, and she was in her third trimester. She wobbled around the kitchen picking up beer bottles. Andre was sitting at the dinner table, face down, and passed out. He had been drinking heavily. She just stood there looking at Andre for a while. She shook her head in disgust. Patricia was tired of Andre. She planned to get out of the house, away from Andre. This time, she would not return.

She knew it was never good news when he drank like that. She went into the closet and got her going-away bag. It contained almost all her belongings. Patricia dropped her keys, and Andre jumped up. Patricia had reached the door and was standing there with it open. Andre asked, "Where the hell are you going?" Patricia starts to shake. She did not know what to say. Her first thought was to make a run for her car, but in her condition, he would probably catch up to her. The idea of her escaping stayed in her mind.

Patricia was packed and ready to go. She had finally decided that enough was enough. She had planned on leaving Andre if he threatened her or their unborn child in any way. She had to think fast and said, "I have to go to the medical facility to get checked out. I am pregnant, Andre, remember?" Andre said, "You better bring your ass back in here, girl! Don't make me come after you." Patricia knew her escape plan would probably not work at that time. However, she felt she might be able to wait him out. After all, Andre was drunk.

She was hoping he would fall back to sleep, giving her another chance to escape. She came back into the house and placed her bag right near the front door. The closet might have been too far away and would impede any escape attempt. Andre stood up and said with slurred speech, "Yeah, but how do I know it's my baby? Shit, the way you've been running those damn streets with those two whores makes me wonder. I have been following your ass, so I know you still hang out with them. Does Club Elegance ring a Goddamn bell?" Once again, Patricia defended her friendship with the girls by saying, "Andre, I told you, we practically grew up together and…"

Andre cut Patricia off and said, "I don't give a shit! I told you I do not want you with them, but you don't want to listen to me." Patricia said, "Andre, how can you say you are not sure if you are the father? That is a terrible thing to say to me. All you have to do is count back to when you viciously attacked me and raped me. Andre, you were my first and I never had sex with anyone!" Her stepfather molested her, but he never had sex with her. "I never raped you bitch. You are my wife and belong to me, so I can do whatever I want, you fat slut! Like I said, I know you've been doing other brothers. I am not stupid. Shit, that baby might be the mailman's or the damn garbage men for all I know!"

Patricia had reached a point where she would leave no matter what. She knew she needed to get out of there before things got too hot. She was thinking perhaps she waited too long after all. She picked up her keys and looked toward the door where her bag was. She was looking around for something to protect herself with. She was not going to take another beating from Andre. She felt it could jeopardize her unborn baby. However, she was not going to take his disrespectful and psychologically abusive comments.

Patricia's mindset was in "fight or flight" mode. Patricia said, "Andre, I don't have time for this. I need to go get checked out. This is important if I am going to have a healthy baby." "I do not care about an appointment! Now sit your ass down and shut up. You are not calling the shots here," Andre said, cutting Patricia off. Patricia defiantly said, "I am getting ready to leave!" Patricia managed to reach the door. She picked up her bag and opened the door. Andre rushed over and slammed the door, nearly taking Patricia's arm off. Patricia's eyes widen as she now knows she is in big trouble.

She is uncertain about how to escape her condition, and aside from her limited martial arts skills, she lacks a means to protect herself. She looked around briefly to see what she could use as a weapon, if all else failed. She didn't know if she would be able to fight back, being in her current condition. She believed she could talk him out of attacking her. "Andre, please don't hurt me." Andre began pushing Patricia back towards the couch and said, "I said sit your fat ass down!" Patricia sat on the sofa. She was scared, but she felt she had to talk to Andre about what had been inside her for so long, even at the risk of getting beaten by him.

Patricia was also worried about him raping her again, even in her condition. Patricia calmly said, "Andre, we need to talk." "Talk about what?" "Andre, we need to discuss this marriage." She thought if she was going to get a beating anyway, she was going to tell him how she felt. She thought that maybe standing up to him would give her the confidence to do so. Patricia yelled, "I can't take this shit anymore! I don't know, I thought you would change, but you will never change." Andre said, "Bitch, I don't know what you are talking about!"

Patricia finally said, "Andre, I want out of this marriage." Andre kicked over a chair and said, "You are not going anywhere whore! There is no place for you to run and no place for you to hide because I will find you. You are going to be my wife, "Until death do us part," just like you said in your wedding vows." Patricia was starting to get bolder and angrier. She was prepared to fight her way out of there if she had to. She wasn't sure the fighting techniques Vanessa had taught her would be sufficient to take Andre down, mainly because she was pregnant. She wanted to get to the kitchen so she could get a pot, pan, or skillet.

A butcher's knife was certainly not out of the question. Patricia said, "Andre, you need to get some help. With your drinking," Andre goes into the closet and pulls out a small black bag. He sits back down on the couch right next to Patricia and places the black bag on the coffee table. He then opens the black bag, takes out a revolver, and says, "This is my help right here bitch!" Suddenly, Patricia was frightened again. She was staring at Andre, who was not very stable, with a gun. She not only feared for her life, but she also feared for her unborn child's life. She began to think she might not live to see the next day.

She wanted to at least try to calm Andre down. She felt that might be her only chance to get out of the situation. Things are not looking too good and appear to be going from bad to worse after Andre dumps some bullets on the table. He starts standing bullets upright on the table while saying, "You see this revolver holds six bullets. This first one is for your ugly ass. This second one is for your punk-ass father. This third one is for your bitch-ass mom. This fourth bullet is for your ugly-ass friend Yvette. This fifth bullet is for your dumb-ass friend Vanessa. Shit, I should bust two in her ass!"

Andre does not put the sixth bullet aside, but instead, he loads it into the revolver and spins the chamber. He calmly asked, "Patricia, you down for a little game of Russian roulette?" Patricia replied by saying, "Andre, please stop playing with that thing and put it away." Andre ignored Patricia and said, "Last, but of course not least, this sixth bullet is for me. That's right, you fat-ass whore, I am not afraid to swallow one of these." Patricia continued to plead with Andre, saying, "Come on, Andre, please stop because you are scaring me now."

Andre appeared to be on a mission and completely ignored Patricia as he put the gun to his head and said, "You don't think I will do myself? Andre stands up and paces back and forth with the gun still pointed at his head. Patricia gets up and slowly walks towards Andre. She is risking her own life and the life of her unborn child to prevent Andre from blowing his head off. Andre pulls the trigger four times, and there is a distinctive click each time. Andre looks Patricia right in the eyes and says, "I've got two more chances to do this. One will take my ass out." Andre pulls the trigger one more time. Fortunately, there is just one more click.

Patricia continues to slowly walk towards Andre. She gets close enough to hold out her hand in hopes that Andre will just hand the weapon over to her. Patricia then said, "Andre, please give me the gun. I love you and I don't want to lose you. I mean, think about our baby." Andre pointed the weapon at Patricia and said, "Don't come any closer! This one will not just click. And you better believe I will blast your ass first!"

Patricia wisely does what she is told. She slowly and carefully backs up. Andre said, "You want to leave me just like those other two bitches. I know where they both are, and I planned to take them out too. I have a couple of slugs for their asses, too. I think I will do them before I do myself. I made the mistake of letting them go, but I am not letting you go anywhere. No way! If you go, it is going to be in a body bag." Patricia felt her best defense at this point would be to try to con Andre and to lie her way out of the situation. She was not sure anything she said would get through to him because he was so drunk. He continued slamming down beers even through all that was happening.

Andre managed to hold his beer in his left hand while holding off Patricia with the revolver in his right hand. Patricia said, "Andre, I am not leaving you. I would never leave you. I told you I love you, baby." "You are lying to me bitch! Don't try to play with my mind. No other man will do what I do for you. And no other man would want your miserable, fat, pregnant ass. So, if you want to leave, be my guest." "Andre, I am telling you the truth, I swear." Andre put the gun on the coffee table. He walked away from it but then paused right in his tracks. He turned around, picked the gun back up, and put it in his waistband.

Andre pointed his finger at Patricia and said, "I tell you what. You want to leave me, you ungrateful slut? I will go pack your shit!" Andre left for a while and went to the bedroom. Patricia made a mad dash for the kitchen phone. She knew that the emergency services could track that number if she could not finish her call. She dialed nine-one-one and barely above a whisper, said, "Yes, I need help here because I think my husband wants to kill me... Yes, his name is Andre Robinson, and he has a gun... Please hurry! She hangs up and dials her parents' house. Charles answers the phone.

Patricia continues to talk low, nearly whispering, and says, "Daddy Andre is at it again…Yeah, please hurry, he has a gun!" Suddenly, Andre's arm reaches around the wall and grabs Patricia, startling her. Andre asks, "Who the hell are you talking to?" Patricia said, "My father, Andre. I can still talk to my parents, right?" Andre said, "No bitch! And he better not come over here to pick you up unless he wants a cap busted in his ass. I said you are not leaving, and I meant that shit." Patricia said, "Andre, I am a little confused now. I thought you said you were packing up my shit so I can leave."

Andre slammed down another beer and said, "I changed my mind, so go sit your ass down." Patricia was hoping Andre would let her go. Now she felt she could become Andre's hostage. The police were definitely on the way, and she thought Andre might decide to go out in a blaze of glory, taking her and the baby too. She had a bad feeling about how the entire situation would unfold. She did not believe Andre would go peacefully this time. She was still thinking of a way to escape from Andre. Andre yelled at Patricia and said, "Sit!" Patricia quickly sat down, still looking for a weapon.

Patricia wished she had grabbed a knife or something when she went to the kitchen to call the police. However, a knife or weapon was not on her mind at that time. Besides, she would have been bringing a knife to a possible gun fight. Andre said, "I think you forgot your most important wedding vow. Remember when you stood up there and said, "Until death do us part?" I believe in that vow. Those other two whores I married forgot about that vow, and so did you." Patricia could not sit there and listen to Andre talk trash.

He kept making her madder and madder. She had planned to ignore him, hoping he would calm down. Usually, he did not force her to listen to him for extended periods. For her, it was worse than a beating. Patricia looked at Andre with hatred in her eyes and said, "Andre, I think you are forgetting that there are other vows that go with that vow that are equally important. I believe, in fact I know, "To love and to honor," comes before that." "Yeah, right, Patricia, whatever. I said it is the most important one to me because the only thing that will separate us is death," Andre replied. Patricia said, "Look, Andre, I am tired of trying to please you. You don't appreciate anything I do for you."

Patricia continued, saying, "Sometimes you treat me like a queen, and those are our best times together. Other times, you treat me like shit. You are like Doctor Jekyll and Mr. Hyde. Every day I wake up, I wonder which one you are going to be." Andre said, "You need to stop watching all those damn talk shows and reading all those stupid novels. Furthermore, you need to stay away from your two crazy friends, as I told you. They fill your head with all that crap. Your friends and your parents try to make you believe I am some sort of monster, and you feed into that shit."

"Andre, I am starting to believe what everyone was saying to me all along. Not just my friends and family. I am hearing the voices of Officer McNeil, Officer Powell, Gina Perkins, and Doctor Richardson, all at the same time. Andre, you will never change, and I will never have any peace here. I don't want the baby to be born into a volatile environment. The vicious cycle stops here!" Andre got up and walked towards Patricia and got right in her face and said, "Shut up! If my mother talked to my father the way you are talking to me, she would have been picking up her teeth. He taught me to do whatever it takes to control a woman."

Andre continued, saying, "I used to hate it when he hit my mother, but he told me some women need discipline just like a child. Later, when my mother fled with us, I started hating her for leaving my dad. Once I started having relationships, what he told me began to make sense. Maybe these nightmares are him talking to me from the grave. Shit, my father was right all along."

"So basically, your father taught you to abuse women. Is that what you're saying?" Patricia asked. Andre replied, "That's right! He kicked my ass often, too, to toughen me up. He said I wouldn't be a punk, because no Robinson has ever been one. He also said that if I could not control a woman by any means necessary, I am less than a man." Patricia believed things would turn for the better if she could keep on talking with him. She just wanted to watch what she said to him, so as not to upset him. At this point in the relationship, she pretty much knew most of the things that set him off. There were times when a good argument from Patricia calmed Andre down. He would have the opportunity to either verbally vent or abuse Patricia.

Patricia had learned that sometimes if she out-argued Andre, he would simply leave her alone. This course of action was certainly not without risks. On some occasions, the argument would escalate and reach a physical level. She knew that if she could engage Andre for just a bit longer, the police would arrive. Patricia said, "Andre, you need some help badly, and I doubt you are going to get it from that stupid anger management course. You can use some AA intervention too."

"You better not tell me what I need bitch! I need a damn obedient wife," Andre declared. Patricia said, "Andre, I called the police and my father, and they are on the way." She thought maybe if Andre knew the police were on the way, he might calm down and not do something stupid. Andre said, "Big deal, you called the police. I will be right back out, and your dumb, ugly ass will be right here waiting for me, just like always. I told you nobody else wants you, and you know it." Patricia said, "Not this time, Andre. I am pressing charges on you this time. I just can't handle this anymore. I guess maybe then you can get the help you need."

Andre began pacing back and forth once again. He was livid at that point. Patricia knew she had gotten to him. He was agitated, but he still had not physically attacked Patricia. Patricia was growing more confident that she and her baby would be able to get out of this in one piece. She was wondering where the Cavalry was and when they would show up. The problem she saw was that Andre still had the gun in his waistband. He took the gun out but then put it back in his waistband.

She remembered he still had one in the chamber, but there were still plenty of bullets on the table. Patricia's thoughts of Andre going out in a blaze of glory were beginning to look like a possibility. "You will pay for all the shit you put me through. I can assure you of that, you ugly-ass bitch," Andre said as he continued to pace the floor. Patricia was shocked that Andre would believe she put him through hell, so she said, "Andre, the shit I put you through?" Andre said, "Yeah, you heard me, you ungrateful bitch!" Patricia had heard enough and refused to let Andre think he broke her.

Patricia boldly stood up and said, "I will not live in fear of you, Andre. Moreover, I am not a bitch, whore, or any of the negative terms you address me as. I am a strong and beautiful black woman. Now, I am going to wait for the police to get here, and I am going to gather my things and get the hell out of here. When you get out this time, I will not be coming back. I don't want this anymore, so I am moving on, Andre." Andre slapped Patricia back down on the couch. At this point, sirens could be heard approaching the house, and Patricia was relieved. She stood back up and said, "I have taken your best shots, Andre, but you have not and will not break my spirit. The Lord has taken me through all this, and Andre, I am still standing." Andre grabbed Patricia by the throat and started choking her. Patricia said, barely above a whisper, "Andre, I can't breathe!" Andre only tightened his grasp and said, "I told you until death do us part, and I meant it. So, if you want to leave me, maybe I should kill your ass!" Patricia struggled and fought to get Andre off her, but she appears to be slowly fading out. She suddenly does a palm strike to Andre's face, which causes Andre to loosen his grip. She then does a kick that sends him to the floor. Andre gets up holding his stomach.

Patricia, now in a fighting stance, says, "Look, Andre, I don't want to hurt you, but I am not going to let you hurt me and potentially our baby anymore." "So, you've been taking some sort of Kung-fu bullshit?" Andre asked, breathing hard and holding his stomach. "Andre, I don't want to fight with you. I just want to leave," Patricia says as she continues to stay in the fighting stance. Andre takes the gun out of his waistband and points it at Patricia. Patricia steps back, out of her fighting stance, and puts her hands up. "Andre, you don't have to do this. Just think about the baby, your son. And you would have to spend the rest of your life in prison."

Andre approaches Patricia with his gun still drawn. Patricia grabs Andre's hand, which is holding the gun. They both fall back onto the couch and begin tussling over the gun. Andre takes his free hand and begins to choke Patricia. Suddenly, there is a loud pop. Andre loosens his grip and slumps backward on the couch. Andre grabs his chest and says, "You shot me bitch!" He tries to grab Patricia again. Patricia jumps up and continues pulling the trigger several times as if she wanted to squeeze out some more rounds.

However, there was only one round loaded in the gun, so it only clicked. Andre collapses. Patricia screams and jumps around with the gun still in her hand. Officer McNeil, Officer Powell, and several other officers burst into the apartment with weapons drawn. Officer McNeil says, "Patricia put the gun down… Please!" Patricia wisely drops the gun and shouts, "He was going to kill me!" Officer Powell knelt and checked Andre's pulse. She looked up at the other officers and shook her head, indicating there was no pulse. She approaches Patricia with her handcuffs out and slaps them on Patricia's wrist.

Officer Powell sadly said, "Patricia, I know you are pregnant, but I must do this. It is standard procedure to cuff all suspects. You have the right to remain silent; anything you say can and will be used against you in a court of law; you have the right to an attorney; if you cannot afford one, one will be appointed for you. Do you understand your rights, Patricia?" Patricia replied, "Yes, but he was going to kill me!" Officer McNeil radioed dispatch and said, "Dispatch, this is Officer McNeil of the DVTF. Roll rescue to this location for a man down with a gunshot wound."

Officer McNeil continued, saying, "The victim is unresponsive at this time and possibly a one-eight-seven. The response is code three. We have one female suspect in custody." They were all too familiar with Andre beating Patricia from the numerous previous calls. Usually, Patricia was the victim. This time, she was the one standing, and Andre was the victim. After a moment of silence, the dispatcher said, "Confirming the male subject is down?" Officer McNeil said, "That is affirmative dispatch, the male subject is down and unresponsive." Charles arrives on the scene. He sees the yellow crime scene tape being put around the house.

Charles came charging into the house with his Louisville Slugger bat and asked, "Did that son of a bitch hurt my daughter?" Charles sees Andre lying on the floor in a pool of blood and says, "Oh my God, what happened?" Patricia, in shock, continues to say, "He was going to kill me!" Charles said, "Baby, do not say anything else." Officer McNeil and several other officers had Charles drop the stick, and they started moving him rather quickly to the door. Charles said, "Wait! Why are you arresting my daughter?"

Officer McNeil said, "Your daughter is a suspect in the shooting of Andre Robinson. Now you are welcome to come down to the station, but this apartment is now officially a crime scene and therefore off-limits." Two paramedics rush in to attempt CPR on Andre, but it is too late.

CHAPTER FOURTEEN

****

We are now back in Dr. Morgan's office, in the present day, where Patricia has finally told her traumatic story for the first time, while being incarcerated. Patricia was crying like a baby, and there was a mountain of used tissues piled in Dr. Morgan's trash can. "That is pretty much it. Now I am here doing time for it. I have had a baby boy since I have been incarcerated. I named him Marcus," Patricia said as she wiped her eyes.

"Where is Marcus now?" Dr. Morgan asked. Patricia replied, "My parents have been taking care of him. They bring him here so I can see him sometimes. Now I do love Marcus Dr. Morgan, but every time I look at him, I see Andre. He favors Andre a lot. He also reminds me of the vicious rapes I endured. I never told anyone about how he was conceived. Not even my parents. Patricia wiped her eyes and continued saying, "At first, I did not want him to see me in here, but my parents said it was important to try to establish a relationship with him. He is already starting with no dad."

Dr. Morgan said, "How does that make you feel? I mean it seems to me that raising Marcus is going to be a big challenge, of course, knowing what you went through and having him constantly reminding you about Andre." Patricia paused for a few minutes and then said, "Well, I would never take my anger out on him or abuse him, that's for sure. I hope he never experiences or witnesses the violence I experienced or the violence his father experienced. I will raise him right and teach him to respect women and treat them well. The vicious cycle ends here."

Dr. Morgan took a tissue, wiped his forehead, and asked, "How does telling your story make you feel?" Patricia said, "Oh God, Dr. Morgan, it feels great. It feels like I just lifted a huge weight off my shoulders. I guess I wanted to tell it all along but did not know how." Dr. Morgan said, "Patricia, your story was one of the more powerful ones I have heard. Do you feel there are any long-term effects from the abuse, and if so, what do you feel they are?" She looked at the Doctor, sort of confused, and said, "Well, I do have nightmares about Andre coming after me and Marcus."

Dr. Morgan replied, saying, "Your nightmares are probably like Andre's nightmares. They may never go away." Patricia once again gets emotional and starts crying uncontrollably. She said, "I wish they would go away. I am getting used to them, though, and they don't bother me as much anymore. I still feel like it was self-defense. I feel somewhat like Sharon Walker in a way, because Andre is gone forever, and he will never put me or any other woman through this again. I just wish I did not have to be here for it.

After a brief pause, Patricia continued, saying, "I think if the cops had arrived sooner, they would have seen Andre choking the life out of me." Dr. Morgan scribbled some notes down and said, "I see." Patricia was trying to peek at his notes as she asked, "So what is your assessment, or should I say diagnosis of me? Am I crazy?" Dr. Morgan responded and said, "Oh no, Patricia, I think you are fine. Considering what you have been through, I think you are a powerful woman and should be able to get through this. You've just completed the first and most important step in the program by sharing your story. Now, do you feel ready to tell it to the group?

Patricia said, "Yeah, I feel like I can tell it to the world."
Dr. Morgan said, "When would you like to tell your story? I
would like you to have the opportunity to prepare for it if need
be." He looks at his calendar and says, "It looks like I will be
gone a couple of days next week, but I will be here Monday,
Wednesday, and Friday. Patricia thinks for a few seconds and
then says, "Let's make it Monday. I do not want to wait too
long." Dr. Morgan scribbled Patricia's name on his desk
calendar and asked, "Should I pencil you in or ink you
in?" Patricia asked, "What difference does it make?" Dr.
Morgan said, "Well, if I put you down to tell your story, I do
not want to hear that four-letter word come out of your mouth."
Patricia sort of laughed and said, "I am sorry, Dr. Morgan, but
I do curse sometimes." Dr. Morgan remarked, "Yeah, you
curse like a drunken Sailor. However, the four-letter word I am
talking about is even worse around here. P-A-S-S is the word I
am talking about."

Patricia said, "There is no way I would pass. I am so ready to tell my story again." Monday morning came rather quickly for Patricia. As promised, Patricia did tell her story to the group. There was not a dry eye in the joint except for Dr. Morgan's. When she finished, there was a long pause, and you could once again hear a pin drop. Suddenly, the silence is broken with applause. The women give Patricia a standing ovation. Dr. Morgan said, "I hope you all are applauding because it was a powerful story and not because she killed Andre."

Later that day, Patricia was out in the visitors' area. Her Lawyer, an African American female in her forties, and two black prison guards are present. The Lawyer's name is Michelle. Patricia was quite nervous because, although they had similar meetings in the past, this one seemed different. Patricia said, "I hope you have some good news for me. I am tired of being in this hellhole." Michelle said, "I do have some wonderful news for you." Patricia excitedly asked, "What is it? What is it?" Michelle answered, "I wanted to take the opportunity to tell you that you have completed this program and have been scheduled for release."

Patricia was very much speechless. She sat there with the two guards on either side of her, with her mouth wide open. She could not believe what she was hearing. Indeed, she knew she was not dreaming because most of her dreams were nightmares. Michelle continued and said, "There was also some new evidence that came up. It seems Andre liked to videotape you and him in the house. Several small video cameras were found throughout the house. When they accessed his cell phone, they found footage with some of the beatings and the rapes.

Michelle continued, saying, "Ironically, he was rolling tape the night he was killed. Turns out the Precinct had the tape all along in their evidence locker. The officer who booked it in was killed in the line of duty a short time before you went on trial. Therefore, the evidence was never turned over." Patricia stuttered but finally got the question out. She asked, "Released from the program or released from prison?" Michelle said, "Actually, you will be released from both. You have already completed the state-mandated program. The incident is being called self-defense. You will be receiving a pardon from Governor Walsh. He insisted on being a part of this.

Michelle continued after a brief pause, saying, "Patricia, you will be fully exonerated. Now, you will be receiving some more treatment or counseling on the outside, but at least you will be doing it as a free woman." Patricia started to cry and said, "Oh my God, that is so great! Praise the Lord! Hallelujah! I can't wait to see Marcus, my two best friends, and my parents." Michelle said, "I am very proud of you. You deserve this. Congratulations." Patricia paused for a moment and then said, "Wait a minute. You did say a tape, right? Do they know if the footage turned up anywhere else, like maybe YouTube or online?"

Michelle said, "There was no evidence of any other tapes or videos at this time. However, we did not know about this tape either, so you never know." Patricia was worried about that possibility, but only for a few minutes. The bigger picture was that she was getting ready to be released from the prison facility. That was all that mattered to Patricia. In this moment, nothing can take away from that. She probably would not have cared if there were a naked picture of her on every billboard in the city. She was getting ready to go home a free woman with time served.

Patricia felt compelled to thank Dr. Morgan and Carol for helping her open up. She would be prepared to thank all the women in the program who told their stories. Two days later, Patricia was in the Evening Scope news program studio. Governor Walsh, a middle-aged Caucasian man, was present. Mayor Lindsay, a middle-aged black man, was present. Dr. Morgan was present. Patricia and her Lawyer were present. Last, but certainly not least, Robert Cassidy was present. Robert was the news program host. He is a Caucasian man, about thirty-five years old.

Robert looks into the camera and says, "Good evening, I am Rob Cassidy, and this is the Evening Scope News Program. I have lots of guests on my panel tonight, so I will get right to the intros. Tonight, my guests include Governor Walsh, Dr. Morgan from Hanford Women's Correctional facility, along with two women who were just released from that facility. Their names are Patricia Robinson and Carol Witherspoon. Their Lawyer is well-known, of course, and her name is Michelle Thompson. And of course, Mayor Lindsay, who I assume is making a cameo appearance.

Robert continues, saying, "I guess I will start with Dr. Morgan. How successful do you feel this state-mandated program will be?" Dr. Morgan said, "I think the program has great potential. I mean it is a fairly new program for our facility, so I can't give you any official numbers or statistics. That being said, it has been successful in other states and facilities." Robert Cassidy said, "What do you feel will be the key to making your program more successful than other rehab programs? We all know that many of these programs fail." Everyone on the panel looked at Robert in shock.

Perhaps going on Robert's program was not such a good idea. Robert liked controversy, which gave his program high ratings. He was known to stir up a few pots and ruffle a few feathers. Dr. Morgan said, "Well, I am sure you would agree that we cannot just lock up criminals without giving them some sort of extensive and intensive rehab. Prison alone will not address the physical and psychological trauma many of these women have endured." Robert Cassidy said, "What do you tell skeptics like me who don't believe any program will help these criminals?

Robert paused, looked around the table, and continued, saying, "Why should society live in fear of these pedophiles, rapists, and serial killers you all insist on putting in these programs and releasing?" Governor Walsh said, "Our prisons are already full. We continue to spend millions of dollars building more prisons. At the current rate, we will have twice as many prisons as schools and colleges. That puts a heavy burden on our state. We believe it is crucial to identify and integrate programs like this into our system. Hopefully, we will be able to rehabilitate and successfully return prisoners to society."

Robert Cassidy shuffles some papers, looks over to Patricia and Carol, and says, "Now you two women were tried and convicted in a court of law for taking the lives of your husbands. Now I think that is murder. Would either of you care to comment?" Patricia cleared her throat, pulled her chair up closer to the table, and said, "Yes, I would like to speak on that." "Now you are umm…. Carol, right?" asked Robert.

Patricia gave Robert the meanest stare-down and said, "No, it is Patricia! I would like to say that you left out one crucial piece of information. They were our abusive husbands. We've paid for our actions, and now we are ready to move on with our lives. This program helps women like us to cope with the mental anguish and pain we feel for what happened to us. Many of us were imprisoned by our husbands for many years. In a lot of cases, when a woman kills her abusive husband, it is in self-defense."

Robert pauses for a moment and then says, "Well, allow me to be the devil's advocate for a minute and ask you both that age-old question. And I know you have probably answered it or heard it on numerous other occasions. Why don't you just get out of the relationship? You know, move on." Carol said, "It is not always that easy, Mr. Cassidy." Dr. Morgan could see that by their expressions, Carol and Patricia were getting hotter with every one of Robert's questions. Dr. Morgan knew it would not be long before Patricia went off on Robert live on National television.

Dr. Morgan knew she would not bite her tongue for long, so he said, "There are many reasons women stay with their abusive husbands. Some believe their husbands will change. Their abusers psychologically brainwash some. Many have nowhere else to go and nobody else to turn to. The psychological abuse can have lifelong effects. I have seen victims whose state of mind could be compared to a shell-shocked war veteran. Those, of course, would not be released. In most cases, many of them would not be in the regular prison system anyway."

Governor Walsh said, "My staff and an independent civilian review board check and review the files of every inmate who has special circumstances for their release. Some are rejected. For instance, there was a third female who did very well in the program but was unable to be released." Robert asked, "Why was that, Governor, if I may ask?" Governor Walsh said, "It was because she specifically went back to her husband to kill him. It was premeditated murder. We are not giving women the green light to kill their partners."

Robert Cassidy started rapping the segment up and said, "I would like to thank everyone for talking with Evening Scope. I wish both of you women luck." He then looks right into the camera and says, "In our next segment, we will be talking to some high-level brass from the police department. We will be discussing the issue of alleged police misconduct within the ranks and on the force. We will be right back after a commercial break, so please stay tuned." Patricia calmly asked, "Are we off the air?" Robert said, "We certainly are, and folks, that is a wrap for this segment."

Patricia, finally able to speak freely, asked, "What the hell is your problem?" Dr. Morgan knew exactly where Patricia was heading with this discussion. He shouted, "Patricia, no!" Patricia said, "Well, he just demonized us and disrespected us on national television. We have already been through enough bull…" "Patricia!" Dr. Morgan yelled once again to prevent Patricia from completing the curse word. "Crap!" Patricia continued. Robert Cassidy said, "Hey, I am just doing my job. Those were tough questions that needed to be asked.

Robert continued, saying, "Now, I am sorry if I offended you, but this segment is over. The network will be returning from commercial break in forty-five seconds." Carol started pulling on Patricia's arm and said, "Come on, Patricia, let's just go. He isn't even worth it." Dr. Morgan gathered his papers and said, "Yeah, let's get going. We do not want any trouble." Governor Walsh, Michelle, and the Mayor walk off the set and exit the studio. Dr. Morgan walks out with Patricia and Carol. It was as if he knew it was not over between Patricia and Robert.

Carol knew Patricia well, too. Dr. Morgan was on one side of Patricia, and Carol was on the other. Suddenly, Patricia turned around and headed back towards the set. She wanted to curse Robert out. Dr. Morgan and Carol grabbed hold of Patricia and escorted her out. The police officers arrive for the next segment and are seated at the round table. Robert Cassidy adjusted his tie and said, "I am certainly glad to see you guys. In this case, a cop was around when you needed one. I thought I was going to have to call you up to the set a little sooner. I bet that one there will end up right back in prison. She needs some help."

As Dr. Morgan was leading Patricia away, he said, "Patricia, you must learn to control that temper. If you don't control your temper, you are going to continue getting yourself into trouble." Carol agreed with Dr. Morgan and said, "Yeah, he is right, girl. Don't be tripping so much."

CHAPTER FIFTEEN

****

It is about six months later. Patricia is now at a battered women's shelter. Ironically, it is the same battered women's shelter that Gina Perkins runs. This time, she is there as an official spokesperson. There are about twenty or thirty women in a large room of the facility. It looks like a hospital emergency room waiting area, as many of the women are in bad shape. Carol is on the stage with her. Patricia's mother, father, two friends, and Marcus are all in the audience to show their support for Patricia.

Patricia and Carol are making their closing statements. Patricia said, "Remember what I said tonight. Every fifteen seconds, a woman is abused in this country. Domestic violence is one of the leading causes of injuries to women aged fifteen to forty-four. There are over two thousand women in prisons and correctional facilities for killing their abusive husbands. So, in many cases, we believe we can't get out of an abusive relationship. Well, I am living proof that the alternative is a lot worse than anything you will encounter if you leave."

Carol added, "Please do not become a statistic or victim of domestic violence. Make a change in you and your children's lives. Remember, he is not going to make a change, so it will be up to you." As the women clapped, Gina went up on the stage. As she clapped her hands, she said, "Thank you, two, for coming out and inspiring these women. Your stories were very inspirational." The women gave Carol and Patricia a standing ovation. They stood there clapping for several minutes.

Gina raised her hand, and the women stopped applauding and took their seats. Gina continued and said, "I have good news for all of you. Patricia has been kind enough to bring us copies of her best-selling novel titled 'Deceptive Vows.' She will be at the back table afterward to autograph some copies. I read the book, and it is certainly a wonderful and informative book. I think it should be required reading for all domestic violence victims." Patricia said, "My agent told me that there are several production companies that are interested in making this book into a movie or Lifetime television program."

Again, there is a standing ovation and applause. The women are treating Patricia as if she were the First Lady. Patricia continued and said, "They all want to change the title to 'A scorned woman,' but I told them I like 'Deceptive Vows' better. Hey, as long as they tell the story like the book and compensate me fairly for it, I don't care if they call it 'Shitty Vows!' The women all think that is funny. However, they know Patricia is joking.

Patricia went on to say, "No, seriously, this goes beyond the money, fame, and glory. Now I do feel fortunate to have all this success. However, I still have a mission. I promised myself to stay focused and grounded, with military-like diligence towards that mission. That mission is to bring awareness to this issue and save lives. At this moment, I want to introduce you to some of my friends and family. This is my father, Charles; my mother, Donna; my son, Marcus; and finally, my two best friends in the whole wide world, Yvette and Vanessa. One other person, whom I have already thanked, is Dr. Morgan. And, of course, I mustn't forget to congratulate Gina Perkins. I owe so much to all of them."

The women give Patricia and Carol one last standing ovation. Patricia, Carol, and Gina walk to the back, where there's a long table and two chairs set up. There's also a box of Patricia's books. Carol doesn't have a book out or a movie deal in the works. Patricia brought her along for moral support and to assist with the motivational speaking aspect of the book signing. Carol was an outstanding speaker. On the way back to the table, the women in the audience reached out to shake Patricia and Carol's hands.

Many of them give Patricia and Carol hugs. Patricia sat at the table with Carol, and the women all lined up to get their autographed copy of Patricia's book. As Patricia started to autograph books, Carol said, "Well, gee, I sure hope I can get a book or movie deal." Patricia said, "Maybe you will and maybe you won't. But what matters is that we stay focused, with our mission and objective always driving us. Our mission is to continue saving lives, one victim at a time. Speaking of mission, I have also decided to get closer to God. This whole ordeal has opened my eyes, and I realize God has blessed me.

About a month later, Patricia was at the Fresh Start Domestic Violence Center. This was a brand-new domestic violence shelter that Patricia and Carol opened. She was there with Carol, Yvette, Vanessa, and Gina. There are also plenty of news cameras and neighborhood people present. In the front, on the lawn, there is a huge banner that reads, 'Grand Opening.' Patricia cuts the giant purple ribbon that's in front of the entry with some large scissors.

As Patricia, Yvette, Vanessa, Carol, and Gina walk down the long hallway, Patricia said, "Well, I want to thank you all for agreeing to assist me in running my first domestic violence facility. The Fresh Start Domestic Violence Center will be the first of hopefully many. I look forward to working with all of you. Now let's get to work!" The women all have a group hug and are both jubilant and emotional. Patricia is at the famous Hollywood Theater. It is about two years later. She steps out of a limousine dressed to kill. Charles, Donna, Yvette, Vanessa, Gina, and Carol are also there. They all accompany Patricia as she walks toward the red carpet.

Patricia stops and looks up at the movie marquee, which reads, 'Deceptive Vows.' There was an all-star cast that starred Angela Bassett, Denzel Washington, Janet Jackson, and Morgan Freeman. Numerous other big names were present, including Halle Berry, and it was expected to be the summer's first major blockbuster. The movie would closely follow Patricia's novel version. As Patricia just stands there for a moment, tears begin to flow down her face. After all, she had been through hell, and she never expected to have so much good come out of it.

Patricia pulled out a tissue and wiped away her tears as she continued their way down the red carpet. There are cameras flashing and news cameras rolling. There are also lots of people standing outside the barricaded area watching. A lady, who is on the red carpet interviewing the celebrities, stops Patricia. The lady is somewhat short, black, about 30, and well-dressed. "Hello, Patricia. My name is Rhonda from the "It's A Wrap" Magazine. How has all this sudden attention and fame affected you, and what are your plans for the future?" She asks.

"Well, I must say it's overwhelming. But, first and foremost, I plan to continue to thank God and put him first in my life. I will continue to support my family and friends since they have always been there for me. Patricia continued, saying, "I plan to open some more Fresh Start Domestic Violence Centers, and I plan to continue being a spokesperson for domestic violence survivors."

Patricia smiled, looked at her parents and friends, and continued. "I guess we will all be taking a nice vacation soon, too." "Sounds great! So, do you plan on doing some more books on domestic violence, since this one was successful in becoming a best seller, and now a film?" Asks Rhonda. "Well, I hope so. I think it's a great way to reach millions of survivors and at-risk women. I mean, the sky is the limit. I may even do some theatrical plays and tour the country with them." "Patricia, thank you for the interview, and best of luck to you," Rhonda said, with a nod and a smile.

About a week later, Patricia and Yvette were walking toward a facility. There were two huge black guys with them, who were Patricia's bodyguards. Patricia and Yvette stopped briefly to read the large sign, which said, "Woman's Self Defense." Patricia shakes her head in amazement and says, "This is wonderful! I can't believe she actually pulled it off!" When they walk inside, they see Vanessa and Officer Powell in karate uniforms leading a roomful of women through kicking and punching techniques. Young girls and teens are also present.

Vanessa tells her students, "Partner up and practice punching, striking, and defensive techniques with my new assistant, Officer Powell." She nods her head at Officer Powell to confirm she wants her to take over the class. She then signals for Patricia and Yvette to come forward. They all head back to the office. Patricia, Yvette, and Vanessa have a group hug. "So, you finally got your Karate school," said Patricia with a big smile. "Yeah, and it looks good, girl!" Yvette added. "Thanks. Who are these guys?" Vanessa asked. "Oh, these are two of my bodyguards, Richard and Big Mike," Patricia answered.

"Why didn't you put me on your security detail? I've been your security detail since we became friends anyway," Vanessa said jokingly. They all laugh, including Patricia's bodyguards. "You guys are going to join us, right?" Vanessa asked. "No, not today, but we will soon," Yvette responded. "Okay, Yvette, I am going to hold you to that. Patricia, I know you are super busy now, so I understand if you can't make it. Now, I need to get back to my class. Hopefully, we can meet up again soon. Patricia, thank you so much for helping me get this place. I appreciate you," Vanessa says as she hugs Patricia, then Yvette. "We're going to get back to our dance routines too... Eventually," Yvette says, sounding doubtful.

Several weeks later, on a Sunday, Patricia was in church, seated in the first row. She was there with her parents, her son Marcus, Yvette, Vanessa, Gina, Carol, and finally, her new man, Kenneth. Kenneth is a 28-year-old, tall black man. He is dressed to kill, in a nice suit. The church is full of people. The large choir is seated on the stage behind the podium. The preacher, a fifty-year-old black man, is standing at the podium. He says, "So, no matter what you are experiencing in life, God will be there for you.

The Preacher continues, saying, "As long as you believe in him and dedicate your life to serving him. Patricia looks at her parents, Kenneth, and smiles. The preacher's words resonate with Patricia. "Now, may all my newly baptized members stand," the preacher said while raising his hands in an upward motion. The whole front row stood, which included Patricia, Kenneth, her parents, her son, her friends, Carol, and Gina. The entire congregation gives them a thunderous ovation. "Now, will you all stand for songs from our wonderful choir?" The preacher asked. The choir and congregation all stand. The choir and congregation sing 'Amazing Grace.'

FINAL THOUGHT

****

Many laws concerning domestic violence changed in the nineties after the now-infamous O.J. Simpson trial. New laws were introduced to better protect victims and give law enforcement more authority when investigating domestic violence cases. An arrest can be made immediately if a victim shows any physical or visible signs of abuse. No questions asked. Over recent years, additional laws have been enacted, yet domestic violence remains a significant issue in today's society. If you or someone you know is in an abusive relationship, contact your local law enforcement, social services, or the National Domestic Violence Hotline **(1-800-799-SAFE)**. It could be a matter of life or death.

ABOUT THE AUTHOR

****

Gary Tavares was born in New York on March 9, 1965. He faced tough times when he and his five siblings were abandoned by their parents. He was no older than four years old. They were all placed in a foster home in the Bronx, New York. The six of them stayed together, but foster parents raised them. Their biological parents were never found.

Growing up, Gary had four different sets of parents altogether. Three sets of foster parents were involved, and the fourth set adopted me. He is no stranger to abuse, as his first foster parents mentally and physically abused him. Fortunately, the foster agency had great social workers, counselors, and child psychiatrists. In 1993, Gary discovered he had the gift of writing. He immediately began taking courses in creative writing to sharpen his newfound talent.

At first, it was a way to channel his energy and escape the realities of life. Later, he decided to use this gift to educate others and do something positive for our communities. He started out writing educational plays. Between 1995 and 2000, he had all four of his educational plays produced in California. He wrote, acted in, and directed each one. In 2000, he began writing screenplays. He currently has four completed screenplays, including Deceptive Vows (screenplay version). He is working on many others.

This novel, Deceptive Vows, was originally one of Gary's most compelling plays. As a play, it was titled "Until Death Do Us Part." The short film version of Deceptive Vows is award-winning, with ten film festival selections and four awards. It has over half a million YouTube views and more than six thousand "Thumbs-up." Gary's full-length screenplay, Deceptive Vows, is also award-winning, having won Best Drama Screenplay at the Summer in the South Film Festival in Atlanta. He continues to use his God-given talent to educate and save lives.

He has been reaching out to the educational system and communities through his educational work. In 2004, Gary became a Youth Motivational Speaker. He visits schools throughout the Atlanta, Georgia area, speaking to students from fourth grade to high school seniors. In November 2005, Gary started his own business in the Atlanta, Georgia area. He is the CEO and Founder of Tavares Entertainment, LLC. He provides publishing, creative, and professional writing services, as well as developing original works.

www.ingramcontent.com/pod-product-compliance
Lightning Source LLC
Chambersburg PA
CBHW051824020726

47502CB00005B/1610